When I started to write *The Looking Glass*, I intended to create a story about the healing power of hope and love. But as this story developed, a message began to emerge that I had not foreseen. . . .

The Looking Glass is aptly named, for it is about seeing the reality of ourselves—a true reflection of who we are—as well as our distorted view of the shackles of self-doubt and fear that bind us. It is the story of Hunter Bell, a Presbyterian minister turned gambler, and the founder of a gold camp named Bethel (which you may remember was Ethel's hometown in *The Locket*). He is running from the bitter memories of his past, his ministry and, ultimately, from his God.

Venturing into a blizzard to chase away hungry wolves drawn close to his cabin, Hunter finds a beautiful young woman in the snow, wounded by the wolves and half dead with the cold. She is Quaye McGandley, an Irishwoman sold into marital slavery to a brutal husband who then brought her to America against her will. As Hunter nurses her back to health, he finds that Quaye has opened his heart to his greatest fear—that he might love again.

It is my hope that you, and those with whom you share my book, might through its message better see the divinity within yourself and the reality of who you are: worthy of love, gentleness, and grace.

With hope,

❄ *THE LOCKET* ❄

"Vintage Richard Paul Evans. . . . Fans of old-fashioned, two-thumbs-up, box-of-tissues tales will love *The Locket*."

— BookBrowser.com

"A heartwarming, three-hanky story."

— *The Pilot* (Southern Pines, NC)

❄ *THE CHRISTMAS BOX* ❄

"This bestseller . . . crystallizes a national yearning for family in these fragmented times. . . . [*The Christmas Box* will] tug families' heartstrings."

— *USA Today*

"The most popular holiday tale since Tiny Tim. . . ."

— *Newsweek*

"*The Christmas Box* has touched something in people who must deal with the loss of a child."

— *The Washington Post*

"A heartwarming story that will appeal to those seeking a renewal of the real meaning of Christmas."

— *Richmond Times-Dispatch*

"An artful blend of fiction and inspirational writing. . . . A memorable tale whose universal message will not fade with the season."

— *The Orlando Sentinel* (FL)

BOOKS BY RICHARD PAUL EVANS

The Christmas Box

Timepiece

The Letter

The Locket

The Looking Glass

The Carousel

For Children

The Dance

The Christmas Candle

The Spyglass

RICHARD PAUL EVANS

The Looking Glass

POCKET STAR BOOKS

New York London Toronto Sydney Singapore

This book is a work of fiction. Names, characters, places and incidents are products of the author's imagination or are used fictitiously. Any resemblance to actual events or locales or persons, living or dead, is entirely coincidental.

 A Pocket Star Book published by
POCKET BOOKS, a division of Simon & Schuster, Inc.
1230 Avenue of the Americas, New York, NY 10020

Copyright © 1999 by Richard Paul Evans

Originally published in hardcover in 1999
by Simon & Schuster, Inc.

ISBN: 0-7434-3099-9

First Pocket Books printing January 2002

10 9 8 7 6 5 4 3 2 1

POCKET STAR BOOKS and colophon are registered
trademarks of Simon & Schuster, Inc.

For information regarding special discounts for bulk
purchases, please contact Simon & Schuster Special Sales
at 1-800-456-6798 or business@simonandschuster.com

Front cover illustration by Dan Craig

Printed in the U.S.A.

ACKNOWLEDGMENTS

I would like to acknowledge those who helped make this book possible: my wife Keri. You are my Quaye. Sydny Miner. It has been a privilege (and a joy) working with you. If it is God's work, so be it. Brandi Anderson. Thank you for your many contributions to this book, your encouragement, and your honest heart. Annik LaFarge, David Rosenthal, and Carolyn Reidy for your continued commitment. Isolde C. Sauer and Jackie Seow for your perseverance. Liz DeRidder, Andy Goldwasser, and James Pervin for their help getting this book into print. The rest of the RPEP crew: Lisa May, Tawna Spoor, and Judy Schiffman. Thank you for your devotion and friendship. The readers who wrote to me after my last book. Thank you. I do read every letter and email. You are appreciated.

I would like to especially acknowledge those women who, for the sake of others still trapped in abusive relationships, shared with me their scars. If you, or someone you know, are in an abusive situation and need someone to talk to, please seek help by calling: 1-800-799-SAFE.

To Laurie Liss

CONTENTS

Contents

"I love thee with a love I seemed to lose
With my lost saints, —I love thee with the breath,
Smiles, tears, of all my life! —and, if God choose,
I shall but love thee better after death."

✳

ELIZABETH BARRETT BROWNING

AUTHOR'S NOTE

In the prologue of my last novel, *The Locket*, I briefly describe the history of a small gold camp in western Utah, called Bethel. Bethel had two lives: its founding in the mid-1800s (and subsequent death at the turn of the century), and its second life during the Great Depression. It was just prior to the Great Depression that *The Locket*'s Esther Huish and her love, Thomas, came to Bethel. *The Looking Glass* also takes place in Bethel, but in 1857, fifty years before Esther Huish's arrival. By the time Esther arrived in Bethel with her father, all of the characters of this book were gone and the only building left standing was the Bethel boardinghouse.

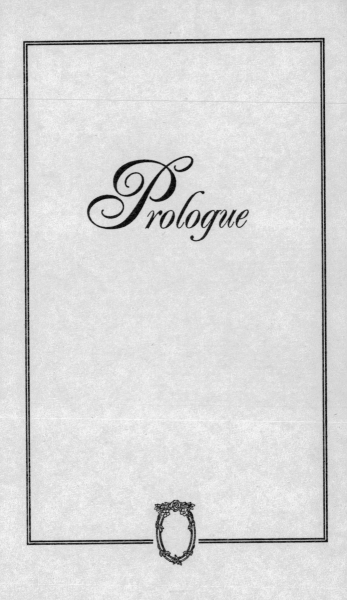

Prologue

There are those who find God in the order of the universe—evidenced in elements as small as atomic nuclei to forces as massive as the cosmic energy that holds galaxies at bay. From Galileo to Einstein to Hawking, the great minds have wondered at the creator of such order; the balance of energy to prescribed laws and constants. While the mathematics of the universe may connote the existence of a supreme being, to me it is that which *defies* math's probabilities—the impossibility of two objects colliding in an infinite void to indelibly alter each other's eternal course. In this there is divinity and an unseen hand.

Through the course of my own life I have come to believe that life is not gifted by the sweep of a clock's hand or the change of a season, but rather, experientially, each experience laid upon the previous, delivering us to a loftier plane. Perhaps this best describes my concept of God—the architect of that ascent and the divine, unseen wind that propels us through the uncharted waters of our own destiny. But salvation, spiritual or otherwise, is not a solitary matter and along such journeys there are companions placed along our travels and travails, fellow sojourners who forever alter our paths and sometimes carry us when we are too weary to carry ourselves. This is the story of such providence.

In 1857, a man named Hunter Bell, a Presbyterian minister turned prospector and gambler run out of the Goldstrike gold camp for card cheating, was wandering among the Oquirrh mountain range in the west desert of the Utah Territory when he chanced upon a streak of gold. He staked his claim and within a month was joined in the area by more than sixteen hundred prospectors. Bell, with sardonic breath, bequeathed his desolate township the name of Bethel—the house of God. It was while secluded in this small, remote township that his path crossed with that of Quaye McGandley, a young Irishwoman from a small hamlet on the other side of the world.

While theirs is a story of redemption, it is, as

well, a love story; they are, perhaps, the same. For it is true that all salvation comes only in and through love. Most simply, the story of Quaye Mc-Gandley and Hunter Bell is the story of two broken people who come together to make each other whole.

CHAPTER ONE

Quaye

There's no love left on earth
and God is dead in heaven
In the dark and deadly days of
Black '47.

❅ IRISH FOLK SONG ❅

It's easy to halve the potato where
there's love.

❅ IRISH PROVERB ❅

CORK, IRELAND, 1847

*C*onnall McGandley trudged wearily across the haze-shrouded countryside, his arms crossed at his chest, his pace pressed against the receding twilight. The chill air smelled sweetly of a distant peat fire and he willed himself to not think of its warmth. Dusk brought a bite to the fog and he had pawned his coat in the last town for the paltry measure of maize he carried in the sack flung across his shoulder. He had walked hungry since dawn with hope of securing relief for his family. There was no labor for hire and his coat had fetched only a couple handfuls of Indian corn from a shopkeeper who chased him out of his store after the transaction. He had encountered few on his journey, just the quiet, deserted bogs and abandoned hovels of a dying nation. The music of Ireland, the land of song, was silenced by famine and the only strains now that filled the air were the occasional piercing wails for the dead—the keening of the banshee.

To the side of the road, behind one of the heaped limestone walls that serpentined across the countryside, a woman crawled on hands and knees through a dank bog, gleaning what had been missed in the last picking, chewing anything that was edible: raw turnips, nettles, and charlock. He turned away. The scene was all too familiar— men and women in the final throes of starvation, their mouths stained green from the grass they ate in a vain attempt to survive. It no longer held curiosity. It no longer held even emotion. It was just the way it was. It would not be long before his own family would be evicted from their hovel, to burn with the fever and madness of starvation or die of exposure. His only son already lay hot with typhus.

It had been two autumns since the mist rose from the sea to cloak Ireland. When the fog lifted, the first signs of the distemper appeared, the stalks bent in the fields, a harbinger of a nation's fate. The blight hit in full the following year, destroying nearly the whole of the island's potato crop. The potato was everything to the Irish poor and the Celts could make anything from the tuber, from candy to beer. The potato was as much heritage as subsistence, but even in the best of times, the potato culture was a precarious existence.

It was shortly before the last harvest when McGandley first discovered the blight on his own meager crop of lumpers—the first lesions on the curling leaves, bruiselike markings that had dropped him to his knees in fervent prayer to St. Jude, the patron saint of desperate circumstance. The family immediately harvested, pared off the diseased portions of the crop, and ate or sold what they could, feeding what they couldn't to the pigs. Then they devoured the pigs themselves. But even the swines' bones which they had boiled, reboiled, then gnawed in hunger, were now gone, replaced only with desperation.

Fifty steps ahead, emerging from the screen of fog, a wooden horse-drawn cart was mired in the mud to the side of the road. A squat, dun-haired man stood calf deep in the mud in front of the horse, pulling at its lines and cursing the animal. It was a curious sight, more so as most farm animals had already been slaughtered for meat. The man saw McGandley and raised a hand to him.

"You, there." The expulsion appeared before him in the frigid air.

As McGandley neared, the man grimaced at McGandley's appearance, surmising him a madman. He had encountered many on the day's travel—men and women, often naked, lunatic with hunger.

"Have ye anything to eat?" McGandley called.

The man frowned. "Not outside my belly." He motioned to the cart. "Can ya lend a hand?"

"If yer wanting to get somewhere, man, ye be better off riding yer buggy on the road, not on the side of it." He stopped an arm's length removed and stared somberly at the stranger. "Are ye English?"

"I'm American."

"Bonny for yah. If ye were an Englishman yer throat likely be cut by now. Likely do it meself."

The American studied the man. "The English been sendin' money to the famine aid."

"Oh have they now? I tell ye, caskets be of more use. There's no famine where there's food. The Brits have stolen it all." McGandley's voice dropped to a more ominous tone. "It is well for ye yer not an Englishman."

The American set aside the horse's lines and took a step toward McGandley. "I have money. Help push me from this and I'll pay ya. I must be to Cobh harbor. My clipper sails at dawn."

McGandley's interest was piqued. In the wake of the famine, more than a million Irish had already emigrated, some to the fever camps of Liverpool or Wales, but mostly to the new world, stowing aboard nearly anything that floated.

"Coffin ships" the seamen called them. There were times that such vessels arrived with Irish aboard but not life.

"Ye be sailing back to Americay?"

The sailor realized McGandley's intent and regretted the divulgence. McGandley did not wait for an answer. "Take pity on our pathetic lot and take us with ye."

"Ya got money?" he asked.

"Not a bleedin' pence."

The American shook his head. "There's no room."

"But, in the steerage, man."

"Along with your typhus and cholera? There's already a million Irishmen at the dock."

McGandley scratched at the lice on his scalp.

"Ye could stow me girl. She's a wee lass."

"I can't, man."

"Ye could if she were yer wife."

The American spit near his own feet. "I don't need no wife," he said, then he turned back to the horse. "Be a good man and lend a hand. I'll pay ya for your trouble."

McGandley stood resolute and the American glanced about helplessly. He had already been delayed the better part of an hour and was no closer to liberating his cart. With night falling and his pockets full of money from the ship passages he had brokered, it was no time to be stranded in Ireland—the horse a banquet, he a bank. The hungry would find him.

"A woman to watch over ya on such a journey would be a blessing," McGandley pressed. "Me girl works hard. Harder than them slaves ye got chained in Americay."

The American still did not respond and McGandley's stomach knotted. He eyed the sailor. He was an ugly man with a wide, ruddy face spiked with stubble, younger than himself by at least a decade, and shorter by a hand.

"What do they call ye, lad?"

The sailor spoke slowly, reluctant to give anything up to the Irishman. "Jak."

"Well now, Jak, she's a lovely lass. A regular colleen. You can do with her what ye like." He gazed at him darkly. "A real man wouldn't pass the offer 'fore he saw the lass."

The sailor stomached the challenge to his manhood and rubbed his forehead as he considered his prospects. A woman would be a blessing on the voyage, even if he were to just abandon her in the waterfront slums of New York. In the darker venues of the city he might even turn her for a profit.

"She's not got cholera or typhus?"

"Healthy, she is."

"If she's homely I'll leave her dockside."

Ignoring the threat, McGandley lay down his sack and moved forward to the task of liberating the cart, his shoes filling with the black mud as he plied his way forward. He rubbed the lean colt's flank to calm it, dropped to his haunches to inspect its breast collar and tugs, then looked to examine the cart. Its wood, iron-banded wheels were buried no more than a half foot in the muck.

"She's a fine pony," he said, patting the horse. He rose, took up the leather lines and stepped off to the side of the horse, then brought the lines down like a whip against the horse's hip.

"Giddout, yer."

The horse's muscles rippled as it strained forward, tearing its hoofs from the mud. The horse advanced with ease from its confinement, pulling the cart straightway from the mire. When the cart was settled on the road, McGandley retrieved his sack of maize, then returned to the cart, offering the lines to the astonished sailor.

"Why wouldn't the blasted beast pull for me?"

A sardonic smile crossed McGandley's face. "Well now, man, if ye be standin' in front of her, where's the poor animal to go?"

❦

The sun was not yet below the horizon when the cart crossed the stone wall boundary of McGandley's clachan. The hamlet, once alive with the voices of children, was mostly deserted as one by one its families were evicted by hunger or landlord. The American halted the cart in front of a thatched-roof cottage and McGandley lowered himself to the ground. A woman, pale and gaunt, with deep wells of eyes, emerged at the sound of their approach. At her side was a young woman who smiled at the return of her father.

"Da."

McGandley did not respond to his daughter's call, and at the sight of the stranger she moved behind her mother. She stared anxiously at the men, instinctively fearing her father's distance and the coarse, leering man who accompanied him. The mother did not ask who the man was who looked on her daughter, but watched silently, as if she were a spectator at a play-act tragedy.

"Come, lass," McGandley commanded.

The girl timidly obeyed, lowering her head as she stepped forward. She was nearly fifteen years of age, fresh in young womanhood with emerging breasts and full lips, her high cheeks ashen with hunger; her long, copper hair spilled over her gaunt and freckled face. She was barefoot, clothed in a high-necked muslin dress purchased two springs previously from the cast-clothes hawkers. The crimson dress, now faded and threadbare, fell crumpled to her forearms and left her long legs exposed. She was, as her father had claimed, pretty, more so than the sailor had expected or hoped for. No such woman, young or old, had ever looked on him favorably. She glanced up fearfully at the man, then moved toward her father.

"What do ya call her?" the sailor asked.

The girl looked to her father, fearing his reply.

"Quaye," he said gruffly.

The man wiped his mouth with the back of his hand. "If she was hung for beauty she'd die innocent. What do ya want for her?"

"Passage to Americay for the girl." McGandley looked down at his feet. "Whatever coins yah got jinglin' about for us."

The sailor reached into his trousers pocket and brought out a handful of coin. "What do ya know? Thirty pieces."

McGandley did not look up. He did not share the sailor's amusement.

"I could buy any woman in Ireland for that."

"She's eaten well till recent," McGandley growled. "She'll serve well enough."

The man said nothing, tossed the silver at McGandley's feet, then motioned to Quaye. "C'mon, girl."

Her mother turned away her tear-brimmed eyes, but there was no disagreement. Either way her child was lost to her. Quaye looked to her father in disbelief, but his countenance was hard and resolute. He squatted down next to her. Looking into her eyes, he said softly, "If ye will remember who ye are, ye will find yer way through it." He looked over to the sailor, who watched impatiently. "Now go 'long with the man, Quaye. He be yer husband now."

"Just a moment," her mother said. She pulled from her spindly finger a silver band then stepped forward and placed the ring on her daughter's ring finger, lovingly clasping Quaye's hand in her own. She said softly, "May ye find love to turn it right someday." Then she kissed her gently on the cheek. "Go well, me girl." She breathed in deeply as she stood. As she rose, the sailor stepped forward to claim his chattel, led Quaye by the arm to the cart, and lifted her in, while her parents watched silently. Without another word the man flailed the horse and started off into the darkness with their child, the cart vanishing into the damp fog and blackness.

"*A mhathair ta me norbh,*" McGandley muttered

to the night air, then he slowly turned to his wife, his head falling with his words. "Mother, I am killed."

Quaye did not turn back as the cart carried her away from her home.

CHAPTER TWO

Hunter Bell

"It has been nearly three months since I arrived in Goldstrike. It is a barbarous camp as thirsty for blood as it is for the noble metals. This last week I witnessed a man gunned down in a barbershop and the proprietor did not so much as interrupt the lathering of his client.

I have become proficient at cards and can turn an ace as well as I once turned holy writ. Cards are more profitable than prospecting and more predictable than God. There is more gold to be had from fools than in the entire range of mountains and it is considerably easier drawing it forth."

❈ HUNTER BELL'S DIARY, MAY 29, 1857 ❈

GOLDSTRIKE MINING CAMP,
WESTERN UTAH. MAY 31, 1857

he white-bearded man mouthed a silent prayer as the cards were laid. Hunter Bell discreetly smiled. He fancied the ones who rubbed icons or spoke oaths, made penance to the gods of chance, as it marked them as easy prey—for poker is not a game of chance, but of patience and skill. Even with cold cards, he would take their money.

In his former life, Hunter Bell's sabbaths were spent behind the burled-walnut pulpit of a small but venerable Presbyterian congregation in West Chester on the outskirts of Philadelphia: his evenings were spent in the civilized company of fellow evangelists, men with manicured nails and oiled hair, drinking tea or sipping brandy from crystal snifters as they discussed the finer points of the gospel or the less digestible meat of its tenets. Now, in the dim, kerosene-lit chamber of the Bucket o' Blood saloon, Hunter's company was bad liquor and the darkened faces of miners and gamblers and the tawdry women attracted to the dark realm. It was not lost on him that he had once, in fiery, brimstone-laced sermons, railed against such men who spent their evenings with demon whiskey and face cards, but the devil's lair had come to be his chapel and every Sunday he could be found collecting tithes from his fellow practitioners.

Hunter would not likely be recognized by his former parishioners. His hair had grown long, falling to his shoulders in waved, flaxen locks. His once soft hands were scarred and calloused. His eyes, which had blazed with apostolic zeal, were still piercing, but now framed with the creases of hardship. He looked older than his thirty-four years. He was harder and thinner of waist and hip, but with the broad, muscular shoulders and chest earned from shoveling gravel into a rocker or an ore car when the cards did not pay. But if he would no longer look appropriate behind a pulpit, neither did he fit at the gaming table. In his black, beaverfelt hat he looked more cowhand than miner and spoke more gentleman than either. Though he drawled occasionally, found his tongue more lazy with each new season, it was still a counterfeit dialect and his vocabulary would occasionally slip, exposing himself as one who did not belong to his blistered hands or rough face.

Goldstrike's saloons did not close with a clock, rather by consensus of their patrons. Tonight's game stretched well into the morning as the three men with whom Hunter shared the table were unwilling to cut their losses—their endurance abetted by whiskey and sizable stakes. They would play until they had won back their gold or had nothing else to wager, the latter more likely, as Hunter had managed to accumulate the bulk of the men's fortunes and the current pot held most of what remained.

The man seated across from Hunter was elfen-faced with a long white beard and a frayed mustache that pulled nearly as far outward as his ears. He was the eldest at the table, nearly sixty, and he had spent his life chasing metal in mountains or tables and had been denied at both. The large man to Hunter's right was named Thomas Cage. He wore a buckskin shirt and denim trousers tucked into his boots. He had thin brown hair and thin eyebrows, and had a cigar protruding from a brush of facial hair. His face was flush with inebriation. The third man, named Marcus, was a particularly unsightly Californian with large ears and a thick scar across the bridge of his nose where a knife had nearly taken it off. He spoke little and lost well. He was drawn into the game at Cage's behest as he usually spent his time and diggings at the faro tables.

A plump, sable-haired woman with eyebrows painted on her forlorn face leaned against Hunter's chair, interested in the mound of gold that had amassed with the hand. She wore a pink satin dance-hall dress that now functioned more as corset than apparel, as it had not grown with its occupant and had become, in places, more revealing than was intended by its seamstress.

"Raise five dollars," the old man said, tossing a coin to the center, the action followed by all except the Californian, who mumbled as he folded his cards. "Could've bought a woman with what I lost."

"A blind one," the woman remarked snidely.

Three more cards were dealt faceup. Cage scowled as he lowered a fresh glass of whiskey from his lips. "This ain't hardly potable."

"Spirits o' turpentine," said the Californian.

"You ought pay a man to stomach this poison." He turned to the old man. "Where's Carter tonight? It's ain't like him to miss a hand."

"Miners' council convened on 'count of his nigra problem."

Hunter knew of what the old man spoke. A group of free Negroes had arrived in Goldstrike and filed a modest claim that had just recently begun to produce. When word of their meager success spread, a group of white miners, led by Carter, moved to annex the diggings, driving the men off their claim at gunpoint. There was no mining law in Goldstrike outside of the miners' council and the black men had appealed to the tribunal. It was a moot procedure as the council was made up of white men notorious for their mistreatment of Indians and Chinese and often itself had a hand in taking claims from other races.

Cage smiled. "Damn nigras oughta just move on. You kin bet Carter'll give 'em Jesse."

"You don't believe that a Negro is as entitled to a find as any other man?" Hunter asked.

Cage looked at Hunter quizzically. "They ain't got no right to stake a claim. It's not like 'em nigras were people."

Hunter pushed a short stack of coins into the center. "Raise five. I was unaware that they're not people."

"Bible say they ain't. Ever since Cain slew his brother."

Hunter looked up over his cards. "God proffers the Bible for the divine. The devil for the stupid."

"Check," said the old man.

Cage still glared at Hunter, unable to ascertain whether or not he had just been called stupid.

"The Bible does not condone slavery," Hunter said. "God gave Cain a mark for his protection, not his condemnation."

The old man said, "A nigra's better off a slave.

Them Yanks workin' in factories are slaves, only their master's a foreman and a machine to tend. If they get old or sick ain't no one takes care of 'em, they just thrown out and someone take their place. Might as well just put 'em down like a lame horse. Them plantation nigras got it good. They get old they still taken care of, even if they ain't good for nothin'. Day I stop shovlin' thirty yards a day I like to see who'll give me a pot a beans."

Cage asked Hunter, "Where ya from?"

"Brodie."

"Ain't no man from Brodie. Where ya born?"

"Pennsylvania."

"Thought he sounded like a Jonathan Yankee," Cage said to the other men.

"There will be trouble with this Negro matter," Hunter said gravely. "We will live to reap the pain of it. Maybe die to it."

Cage examined his cards, drank, lit another cigar, then returned to the table's society as if he had been suddenly absent.

"I'll take another card," Hunter said.

Cage slid a card to Hunter then asked, "How d'ya know so much 'bout the Bible anyhows?"

"I read it."

"Round these parts that qualifies ya as a preacher."

"I was a preacher."

All three men looked at Hunter disdainfully. In

Goldstrike he might as well confess to claim jumping or to being a lawyer, as all were held with equal contempt.

"I knew a religious man once," the Californian said. "Shot him."

"Explains yer fancy talk," the old man said. "Mebbe yer luck."

"Maybe," Hunter said.

" 'S'pose Goldstrike's fertile ground fer a preachin' man," said Cage. "Larceny at every wag. 'Cept a miner got 'bout as much use fer a preacher as a snake fer a walkin' stick."

"I didn't come to preach. I came for gold."

"What kind of preacher is you?" the Californian asked skeptically. "Gamblin' and boozin'."

"A fallen one."

"A son of perdition," Cage said. "See your ten. Raise ya five." He tossed a coin onto the table. "Way I see it, all preachers in cahoots with the devil. Where'd a preacher be without sin?"

A smile pulled at Hunter's lips; it was the only assertion of the night he found remotely amusing. "I see your five dollars and raise ten more."

"You ain't like any preacher I seen," continued the Californian. "Say somethin' from the Bible."

"Shaddup," growled Cage. "We're playin' cards." He shook his head at Hunter's bet. "You been bluffing all night. Preacher or no, I ain't never seen a man lie as well. I'll see your ten and call."

The old man reluctantly pushed the last of his stack to the pot.

Hunter looked up from his cards, then smiled at the Californian as he recited a psalm: "Riches make themselves wings; they fly away as an eagle toward heaven." He lay down his cards, a spread of three kings, and looked at Cage. "Finally got a hand."

The old man threw his cards to the table while Cage muttered a string of profanities that made the woman smile. Hunter sat calmly, allowed the curses to run their course, and did not move too quickly to claim his pot. He had once seen a man's overly eager hand pinned down to the table with a bowie knife.

"Any more, gentlemen?"

"Ain't nothin' more to bet," said the old man, pushing away from the table. The Californian likewise stood while Cage looked on in disbelief. "Can't figger out how ya cheated."

Hunter stared intensely at the man. "Are you calling me a cheater?"

As the two men stared each other down, the old man and the Californian backed away from the table. The bartender saw what was coming and lifted a shotgun from behind the bar. "I'll blow the head clean off the first man to fire a gun in here."

The old man said to Cage, "Don't go messin' with a preacher man. 'Specially some son o' perdition."

Without breaking eye contact, Hunter took from his waist his buckskin purse and collected the pot with the rest of the night's winnings, then placed the bulging pouch in the breast pocket of his coat, intentionally exposing the derringer he carried. Sitting in a Goldstrike card game unarmed was the height of arrogance and, to some, warrant enough to kill.

"Bring them all another drink," Hunter said to the woman, leaving two coins on the table. "Something better than turpentine."

Hunter stood, tipped his hat to the woman, and walked out into the cold, darkened street. The night air was cacophonous with the din of crickets and once he was outside the saloon he exhaled in relief. He could handle a gun, but his skill with a weapon was mediocre at best and untested in actual conflict. He had no desire to stake his life on his proficiency. He had challenged Cage because the only thing surer than confronting a man to provoke a shooting in the West was to show a man weakness.

He glanced once more at the saloon to be sure that he was not being followed, then he started walking home toward the Orleans boardinghouse.

The street at night was not unfamiliar to him. He did not sleep well and often walked beneath the midnight moon, even before coming to Goldstrike. But especially in Goldstrike. He did not trust the place. He had lived in more than a dozen camps since his journey west, mostly in the pacific northwest, and Goldstrike was neither the toughest nor the most decadent, but it left him the most anxious. Life was cheap here and if homicide was more common elsewhere, it was not for any reason other than that there were more efficient murderers elsewhere. Outside of Judge Lynch, the law was impotent in the town and, on the rare occasion when a trial was convened, it was without the assistance of lawyers. It was the rule of the vigilantes that if a man they deemed guilty walked free on account of a lawyer's skillful tongue, the lawyer would be hung in his stead or, at the least, be relieved of his tongue. It did not take long for the lawyers to leave town.

Hunter also walked because he no longer had a horse. One morning, three weeks after he had arrived in Goldstrike, he found his horse, a buttermilk-colored palomino, dead in front of the boardinghouse. The horse's death happened to coincide with one of Hunter's streaks of sizable winnings, and even though he could not prove it, he suspected that the animal had been poisoned. It was the kind of deed he would suspect only in Goldstrike, for killing a man was one thing, but killing a horse was downright shameful.

The Salt Lake City tabloids had called Goldstrike "Sodom West" and Hunter had once thought that if God did not destroy Goldstrike soon, He would have to apologize to the former inhabitants of both Sodom and Gomorrah.

He arrived at the darkened boardinghouse, climbed the three stairs to the porch, and went inside. The dining room was dimly lit by a dying kerosene lantern hung near the doorway. Asleep beneath it on a rocking chair sat a pretty, mahogany-skinned girl, her long black hair dangling just above the floor. Isabel Gayarre was the daughter of the boardinghouse owner, Père Gayarre, an irascible Cajun who was rarely seen and avoided when he was.

Hunter crouched next to her. "Isabel?"

She stirred, her eyes fluttered then opened, and she smiled when she saw him. "Preacher, is it morning?"

"No. It's still night. You should be in your bed."

He put his arm around her to help her up and she leaned into him, sighing happily as he walked her down the hall to her room. He stopped at the threshold and would not enter, fearing that her father might see them and misunderstand his intent. She turned back and sleepily moved to kiss him but Hunter placed his finger on her lips.

"Good night, Isabel."

She kissed his finger and smiled as she shut the door behind her.

Hunter climbed the stairway to his own room on the second floor, the last door in the hallway. The darkened cubicle resonated like a saw house with his companions' snores: seven men, tramp miners, each in a small bunk with a bedroll, their life's belongings cached beneath their cots. It was not uncommon to bed so many to a room; he had boarded in a house in Bend, Oregon, where twelve men occupied a single room, three to a bed. He removed his coat and concealed the night's winnings in his blouse, buttoning his shirt up around the purse. He set his hat aside and did not bother to remove his boots as he lay down to sleep.

CHAPTER THREE

Isabel

"Though I continue to rebuff her advances, the boardinghouse owner's daughter is well-dispositioned toward me. At times, hearts are the most traitorous of devices. They tumble headlong and blindly toward obvious dangers while they obstinately protect us from that which would likely do us the most good."

❀ HUNTER BELL'S DIARY, MAY 28, 1857 ❀

$\mathcal{T}$he Orleans boardinghouse was one of Goldstrike's original edifices: a two-story building with a gambrel roof and stone fireplaces on each end of the house. Its walls were erected of exposed, milled lumber. It was considered a boardinghouse of some repute, with oilcloth-covered tables and a superior quality of knives and forks. The place was home and eatery to about fifty men, mostly tramp miners and drifters, with a population that changed on a monthly basis.

The owner, Père Gayarre, was a one-armed Cajun as quick of gun as temper—both sharpened by a life of travail and piqued by necessity of his daughter's beauty. It's been said that "a Cajun don't die, he dry up" and Gayarre looked well on his way to desiccation, his wrinkled face gray as an aging Joshua tree. It was rumored that he had many years previously ridden with the Natchez Trace bandits, a notorious group who terrorized the swampland of Louisiana. There was no way to substantiate the truth of this as he was not given to conversation and would as soon bury a man as confide in him. Gayarre had kept for a time with a black woman, evidenced in the coffee-colored skin and dark eyes of his beautiful daughter, Isabel. The woman had died when Isabel was still a child and now, at seventeen, it was Isabel who maintained the Orleans, cooking and caring for her father as well as the boarders.

It was said of Gayarre that he was among the surest guns in the territory and had not, to the locals' recollection, lost a gunfight, though it was sometimes noted that he had lost an arm in one. It was in Tulsa where a gaming young rustler, brandishing a revolver, made advances to the young Isabel. When she refused him he slapped her and called her a half-breed nigger. It was doubly unfortunate for him that Gayarre was within earshot and gun reach. The Cajun lost one arm in the contest but the rustler took both of his to the grave.

Gayarre was clearly fond of his daughter and the miners took note of it. His reputation with a gun extended as far as his daughter's reputation with a skillet and if the greenhorn miners who came to the house found themselves as keen on the cook as they were on her victuals, it was for only as long as it took the more seasoned boarders to explain to them the way things were. Hunter was the only man in Goldstrike who had spent any time with Isabel, and it was at her advance, not his.

Isabel had watched Hunter with great interest since the first day he arrived at the Orleans. He was a gentleman, but no dandy, soft spoken and polite, his eyes burned from a flame of a different world that she could only imagine and sometimes fantasized he might lead her to. Her fascination with him grew, as well as his mystique, as she learned of his nocturnal habits. Hunter was a melancholy man and plagued with insomnia. Some nights, when he could not sleep, he would sit alone in front of the stone-hearthed fireplace with a bottle in hand and a book in his lap. At times, Isabel would silently watch him from her bedroom through a partially cracked door. One night she saw the fire reflect from his eye and thought perhaps he was pining for a lost love. She came to him that night with tea and honey, sat down next to him, saying nothing until he looked over at her. His eyes were sad and wet and she took his hand; neither of them said a word until the fire died and Hunter walked alone to his room carrying with him the book he had held in his lap and the picture he had tucked between its pages. A book of sonnets and a picture of a small girl. They did not speak of the night the next morning, or ever, but she had not slept the same since and could not look into his face without feeling heat come over her body.

✳

Hunter woke alone in the room; the other men were gone with the sun, rising before dawn to meet their employer's law. As he sat up in the bed he felt the bag in his blouse and remembered the night's success at the poker table. He liberated the purse and spilled its contents on the cot. He never counted his winnings at the table but had estimated them at around six hundred dollars. He counted out the coins and found that he was within ten. One more take like the previous night's and he would be ready to move on to Arizona and then Texas or Mexico. He wasn't certain. He just knew he would leave this place.

He raised himself to the side of the bed and rolled his head to stretch his neck. He pulled his overalls up over his shoulders then descended the stairs to the main floor. The dining room was vacant except for Isabel, who walked out of the kitchen in an apron soiled from the morning's kitchen duties. Her eyes were puffy from the late night and she smiled shyly at him as she brushed the hair back from her face.

"Mornin', Preacher."

Hunter tipped his hat. "Isabel."

She ducked back into the kitchen. He thought for the thousandth time how pretty she was and just as quickly chased away the thought. There were times, his resistance thinned by drink and fatigue, that he had considered allowing her in, desperately wanting someone to soothe his searing loneliness. But the walls he had built around his heart were thick, impervious to alcohol and pretty brown eyes and perhaps thicker than he himself could bring down.

He sat at a table near the fireplace and Isabel soon returned carrying his breakfast, a plate of biscuits smothered in gravy made from bacon drippings and a tin cup of black coffee. Isabel always saw that Hunter had larger portions than the other boarders or an extra biscuit or dumpling at no charge.

"You came in late. It must have been a good night at the tables."

"Exceptional night," Hunter said. He pushed toward her his purse to stow with the rest of his cache in the boardinghouse strongbox. "You should not wait up for me."

"I worry, Preacher."

"Why would you concern yourself about me?"

"In Goldstrike, a man that is too lucky at cards is

not often popular. Or long-lived." When he did not respond she looked toward the window. "It looks like it might rain tonight. Do you suppose they will postpone the war?"

"The war?"

"Have you seen the advertisements?"

He shook his head.

Isabel went to the kitchen and returned with a paper which she handed to Hunter. He read it aloud.

Come All! Come All! The famous bull-killing bear SAMSON will meet DELILAH, the fiercest killer bull ever to leave Spain. Delilah's horns will not be dulled to prevent accident.

"It's been the talk once the advertisements came."

He lay the sheet on the table. "It is a barbarous display of man's savagery."

Isabel smiled. Hunter used words the other miners did not even know and even a rebuke sounded to her like poetry.

"They built that arena just for the war. I thought perhaps we could go together."

Hunter looked into her eager face and she smiled hopefully. There was a dearth of women in the camp and few of those warranted a second look. Even with the threat of Gayarre, not a man in Goldstrike would refuse such an offer. Still, Hunter wavered. She touched his hand, carefully studying his eyes. ". . . Or we could meet somewhere else. You could read to me from your book."

Hunter adjusted his hat as he considered the proposal. He finally asked, "What was the hour of the war?"

"Five o'clock."

"I will meet you at the arena at five minutes of."

Isabel was not sure whether to take his response as rejection or acceptance, so she just smiled and went back to the kitchen. Hunter downed his coffee, then left the room empty as he headed off to work his own meager claim.

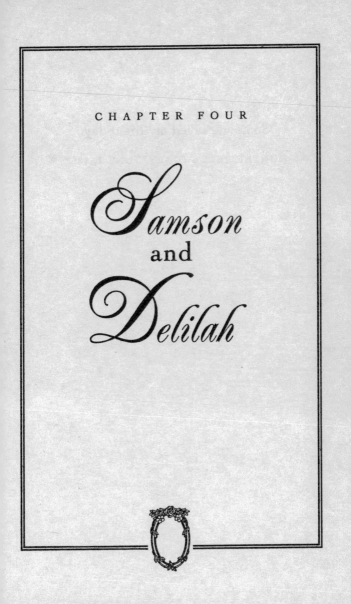

CHAPTER FOUR

Samson
and
Delilah

"Someone saved my life today."

※ HUNTER BELL'S DIARY, JUNE 1, 1857 ※

$\mathcal{G}$oldstrike was in a carnival mood. Nearly the whole of the gold camp's citizenry had congregated at a makeshift arena near the center of town for the bear-bull contest. While cockfighting was common to the saloons and a regular fixture at most gaming halls, game this large was unusual and provoked unprecedented excitement in the town.

The arena, created expressly for the occasion, was about seventy feet in diameter, enclosed by thick wooden planks ten feet in height, the whole surrounded by stacked tiers of benches for spectators. A vanity of women, what few the town offered and mostly from the line, huddled together at one side of the oval with the prospect of leaving with clientele, but were not presently thinking business as they too were caught up in the reverie of the sport. A brass band composed of Goldstrike's miners tortured "The Star-Spangled Banner" amidst the whooping and stamping of the eager miners.

Hunter paid fifty cents to the gatekeeper, climbed the stair into the arena, and looked for Isabel. When he did not find her, he took a seat near the entrance to await her arrival. As he sat, he noticed a man across the arena point to him but he paid it small heed. Such regard was not new to him, in Goldstrike or anywhere else he had camped in the West. He had failed, perhaps refused, to assimilate into the camp's society and he knew that the townspeople spoke peculiarly of him, as it is man's nature to distrust those unlike himself and fear those he does not understand.

In the center of the arena lay the celebrated grizzly bear, Samson. The animal, confused by its surroundings, had earlier charged the plank walls of the arena to no effect but the jeers and hooting of the crowd. Flustered, it sauntered to the center of the arena and lay down. Near the wall opposite Hunter, sequestered in a cage to the east end of the oblique, was Delilah, a twelve-hundred-pound bull advertised of Spanish ancestry. In truth, the nearest the beast had been to the old country was the Baccaro ranch hand that brought it out the day before from Provo, Utah.

At the band's crescendo, the gate was opened on the cage and the bull, incensed at its long confinement, charged out, bucking and tossing its head about, looking for something on which to vent its rage. At the sight of the bear it hoofed a spray of dust into the air.

The bear nonchalantly raised its head from the ground to eye the bull, then resumed its former tranquil position on its side. To the crowd's delight, the bull lowered its head and charged the bear. There was a great collision and the bull gored the bear's chest, rolling the surprised animal to its back. The bear quickly rose to its feet and roared ferociously, its bellow drowned by the crowd's roar of approval, their bloodlust piqued by the sight of blood spilling down the bear's torso.

The bull strutted proudly along the circumference of the arena. Men with bottles or hats in hand leaned over the embankment in an attempt to hit the animal as it passed. Then the bull charged again. This time the grizzly caught the bull and threw it to the ground, holding the frantic animal in its powerful claws.

The struggle brought the crowd to a frenzy and Hunter found himself watching not the animals but the crowd—especially the womenfolk, who whooped and laughed at the bull's plight with such delight as to shame the men. Deciding the humans were the more brutal of the creatures, Hunter rose and stepped back to the top of the arena to resume his search for Isabel.

There was suddenly a loud cry from the specta-tors as the bull broke free of the bear's grasp and bolted as far from the grizzly as their confinement allowed. Then, to the consternation of the crowd, the bull lay down—the fight gone from it. The bear likewise seemed to have no more desire for the con-test and sat back on its haunches.

The disgruntled crowd began hollering. The promoters, who had promised satisfaction, now feared for their own safety and quickly took to end-ing the armistice by goading the bull with long spears until it jumped back to its feet while the spectators nearest the bear threw empty bottles and stones at the beast. One man tossed a pickax.

Just then Isabel stole up behind Hunter and touched his shoulder.

"Preacher."

Hunter turned. Isabel was breathless, her face bent with anxiety.

"What is it, Isabel?"

She took his hand. "Come with me."

He followed her to the top of the stair entrance of the stadium where a mule-hipped Appaloosa was tied. She spoke in hushed, fervent tones. "I over-heard some talking at supper. A man said you've been cheating at cards and the vigilance committee means to fix you."

The report sent a chill through him. The vigilantes did not speak idly of such things. Hunter had been in the town less than a hundred days and could already claim witness to six lynchings at the hands of the committee.

"Do you know the man?"

"He was a tall man. He said he played poker with you last night."

"Cage," Hunter said, cursing himself for his stupidity. Thomas Cage was the acknowledged head of Goldstrike's vigilance committee. The vigilantes were the law in Goldstrike—judge, jury, and hangman—and their tin justice was all too easily bent to their own whims. They felt not only justified in their acts but, in the name of civilization, virtuous in their doings, sometimes posing for group photographs next to their victims. They would be thirsty for blood after the sport.

"He said they're going to leave you stretching hemp right out front of the gambling hall you took him at."

"Did he say when?"

"After the war when everyone's blood is up and they can raise a posse."

Hunter glanced back across the arena toward the men who had been watching him. One of them was looking his way.

"Take my horse, Preacher. I've packed your things."

"My gold?"

"Everything I held for you in the strongbox."

"What of the rest of my things?"

"I gathered everything that was in your room. And I packed some food."

Hunter looked on her gratefully. "I will pay you for the horse." He counted out fifty dollars in gold coin and held it out to her. She took his hand and did not release it. There was a sudden shout from the crowd and Isabel looked toward the arena, then back.

"You best hurry, Preacher. I don't think that bull is long for life." Her voice quaked as she spoke and he noticed that her hand trembled on his.

"Take me with you, Preacher."

"I can't, Isabel."

Looking into his eyes, she took a deep breath and said, "Let me be her."

He looked at her in sadness, and, after a moment when he did not answer, her eyes brimmed with tears. She took a knife from her corset, stretched her ebony hair, cut off a lock, and handed it to him. Hunter closed his hands around the hair as Isabel wiped her eyes.

"Good-bye, Preacher."

Hunter put his arms around her and she pressed her forehead against his shoulder, then gently pushed back. "It is not safe. You must go."

He released her, climbed down to the horse, and mounted it. He tipped his hat to her.

"I will not forget you, Isabel."

She could not bear his gaze and she turned away. He kicked the horse and when he was gone she said softly, "God's speed, Preacher."

CHAPTER FIVE

Flight

"I have fled yet another town. It is a precarious line I walk; one step ahead of the noose and one step behind peace."

❋ HUNTER BELL'S DIARY, JUNE 2, 1857 ❋

$\mathcal{T}$he skies had turned leaden and though there was no rainfall yet, lightning flashed and cracked the darkened heavens and thunder bellowed throughout the great basin of desert. Fearful that the vigilantes had witnessed his departure, Hunter rode slowly toward the Orleans to avoid raising their suspicion. He casually glanced back over his shoulder as he passed behind the boardinghouse, then, once behind the main row of buildings, rode the horse at a gallop toward the east, past the miners' shanties out of Goldstrike.

At the town's outskirts he turned the horse south, riding parallel to the mountains, choosing the shadows of the foothills to the swiftness of the desert. After a half hour of hard riding the skies started to sprinkle lightly and he did not begrudge it. While he had still seen no evidence of chase, it brought him only a small measure of solace. There

were good horsemen and trackers among the vigilantes and fleeter horses than Isabel's. The moment
he sighted the riders it would likely be too late. The
rain would make it more difficult to track him and
the men less likely to follow. The vigilantes were
easily stirred to passion, but that passion was neither deep nor long sustained; they were less likely
to venture this far from Goldstrike in a downpour
when they could be dry in a saloon warming their
feet with fire and their gullets with whiskey.
Unfortunately, he could not be certain of this as
there had not been a lynching in Goldstrike for the
better part of the month. Sometimes bloodlust built
in a community; in his travels he had seen men
unsuccessful in their lynching quest turn on one of
their own to quench their thirst for blood.

The rain grew steady, bouncing off his hat and
spilling over its rim. He removed his hat, took his
poncho from his pack, pulled it over his head, then
replaced his hat. Starting off again, he rode closer
toward the mountains in search of refuge for the
night.

There were reasons other than rain and vigilantes to find shelter. He was on Gosiute lands now
and if he were to climb to the other side of the
mountain he would find their cedar-bark winter
lodges, if not the inhabitants themselves. The small
band of Gosiute had been forced into the desolate

basin by the more powerful Shoshone and Ute, evolving into an eclectic band that survived by accepting the outcasts of other tribes. The barren desert offered poor sustenance and their diet consisted principally of snake and lizard or desert roots with an occasional bowl of red-ant-egg soup. While the Gosiute were not considered fearsome as warriors, the introduction of white man's horses and supplies into the territory provided irresistible temptation and the number of Gosiute attacks on white settlements, evidenced by arrowheads dipped in rattlesnake poison, had escalated in recent years.

The winter before, a small group of Goldstrike's miners, venturing off in search of new finds, had unearthed gold in the area he now rode and foolishly staked a claim on a Gosiute burial site. When the miners were not heard from for a fortnight, the U.S. Cavalry dispatched a patrol and found the camp deserted; picks, shovels, and pans were left leaning ready against the mouth of the mine, as if the whole of the camp had decided to go for a constitutional and never returned. To this day, the miners had still not been heard from or their bodies recovered.

A lone man wandering in the territory might be ignored by the Gosiute, but one could not be certain.

Moving along the shadow of the jagged stone at the base of the foothills he spotted a sizable fissure in its rock face. He dismounted and led his horse by its reins to the mouth of the crevice. The orifice opened to a small cavity in the rock; he dropped to his knees and peered inside, finding it too black to judge its depth. He found a tree branch and probed the cavern for rattlers. When he was satisfied of its vacancy, he crawled inside. The hollow was not large, slightly less space than a man needed to stretch out, but it was dry and he had slept on smaller cots. He tied the horse a distance from the cave and released its saddle, then covered the floor of the cavern with the saddle blanket. Shortly after he crawled into the space, the downfall intensified and the mountains echoed the blistering crack of thunder, followed by the occasional whinny of the Appaloosa. The torrential rain slid off the stone face of the mountain, cascading over the opening of the cave, but it remained dry inside. In the darkness, Hunter pulled his knees up to his chest and closed his eyes. He took Isabel's lock of hair from his shirt pocket and rubbed it between the fingers of one hand. Only then, in the fortress of rock, did he think about Isabel and wish that he were not alone.

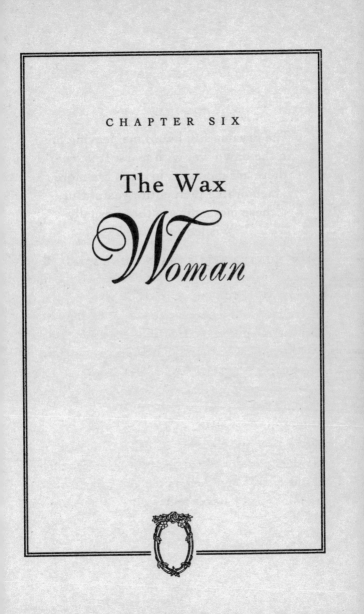

CHAPTER SIX

The Wax
Woman

"The dreams still haunt me, leaving me in the dawn wet with tears. It is true, there are moments in one's life more memorable than entire years. But these moments are those usually wished forgotten."

✳ HUNTER BELL'S DIARY, JUNE 3, 1857 ✳

It was always the same nightmare that haunted Hunter's slumber. Though staged in diverse settings as if to steal unrecognized into his sleep, it was always the same drama, the same woman, the same tragic conclusion.

This night the dream took place in a civilized place, an ornate, richly furnished parlor with brocaded haircloth-upholstered sofas and chairs. There was a round marbled-topped table adorned with a bronze sculpture of the goddess Athena, and another walnut table with a porcelain vase with a bouquet of peach roses. The room had a fireplace without fire, the firebox surrounded by a marble-tiled hearth and an elaborate rosewood mantelpiece. It did not seem peculiar to Hunter that the chamber had no ceiling and was laid wide open, exposed to the night's chill sky.

Hunter's companion was a beautiful woman

with full lips and a delicate face with deep, almond-shaped eyes. Her luminous skin was smooth and clear as porcelain and her sepia-brown hair was drawn tightly back from her face with an ivory haircomb. Hunter and the woman lay close together on a Persian tapestry. The woman was warm and soft and her companionship soothed Hunter's addled mind and he could not think — did not wish to think, only feel her presence.

"I have missed you so," she whispered to him in a voice thick and sweet. Her soft cheek brushed against his. "It is cold, my love. Hold me tighter."

As Hunter lay into the woman, she sighed contentedly and the sound of it coursed through him as a hymn. Suddenly there was warmth at his back.

"The sun . . ." the woman said. As she spoke, the first streaks of dawn rent the night's veil. He was not sure what she had meant, but he knew that he did not like the way she had said it.

". . . I shall leave with the sun, darling," she said and she pressed into him and kissed his neck. He looked at her and saw that she was turning pale, then translucent like wax.

"No. You can't leave me."

Her blanched lips moved. "But I shall, you know."

He grasped her tighter. "Please don't leave me again."

She spoke with resignation—a submission to the inevitable. "Hunter, it is starting . . ."

Hunter tried to spread his body over the woman's, to shield her from the lethal sun, but her skin moistened with the dawn's heat.

". . . I am sorry, my beloved."

A tear streamed down her cheek like the weeping of a candle. Her eyes, wet, became as liquid as the tears themselves, and then they, too, began to melt, the process escalating until within moments she was gone and he, sobbing gently, lifted himself to his knees from the saturated rug, wet with the tallow that had once been his beloved. Beneath him now was only a shadowlike impression where she had lain and a golden ring. Suddenly the air was pierced by the sound of a baby's cry. He lifted the ring and, clenching it tightly in his fist, he looked toward the sun and screamed.

CHAPTER SEVEN

The House of God

"I have ridden two days by horse from Goldstrike into the solitude of Utah's desert. I find it peculiar that I am less lonely in the isolation of the desert than in the bustle of Goldstrike. Loneliness is often heightened by company."

HUNTER BELL'S DIARY, JUNE 3, 1857

*H*unter woke with the echo of his own scream. The sky had cleared from the night winds and the eastern sun now pierced the crevice, illuminating the back wall of the cavern in a jagged streak. His eyes were wet. He reached down his shirt to the chain he wore around his neck and fondled the golden ring it held. It had become a ritual of sorts, but like most rituals, was less of meaning than habit. He climbed out of the cave and gazed out over the desert landscape to the eastern horizon where the Wasatch Range huddled the Salt Lake valley in a stone crescent. He tried to determine just how far south he had ridden.

In fleeing Goldstrike, Hunter had paid less attention to where he was going than where he was running from. In truth it was the way he had lived his life. He had abandoned all in the flight west; everything except the memories which he could not escape.

Hunter had left Pennsylvania four years previously with the intent of putting as much distance between his former life and himself as possible. He headed to the opposite coast, in search of gold instead of God, carrying what few belongings he could not part with: a book of poetry and his diary, and only enough provisions to ensure his survival. He had taken the overland route, traveling with a wagon train from Ohio on the California-Oregon trail. It was during the crossing that he learned the truth of the gold rush from broken men headed the opposite direction.

The prospectors' dreams were no longer; gone were the hopes of coming to the West for a few years then triumphantly returning east to their wives and families overburdened with wealth. The easy gold, that placer metal picked or panned from riverbeds and creeks, was long gone. Now a lone miner could not even count on scrounging up enough ore to fill a stomach with beans. Men scrambled and hoarded, died over small plots of depleted land, and even though the newspapers continued to blaze headlines of California's golden promise, the only ones getting rich were the merchants.

It had been this way for several years as lone prospectors, of necessity, banded together in companies to more efficiently dredge the beds and protect their diminishing finds from the increasing number of bandits. But now even these companies of miners were facing extinction as big, well-funded corporations with hydraulics and dredges moved into the land. Miners were no longer prospectors, but corporate employees of eastern concerns owned by men who had never seen the West or filled their fingernails with its dirt.

Suicide was widespread. Where there was once no need for jails, the prisons were now crowded to capacity and hangings so commonplace that even some of those to be lynched appeared to regard their fate with nonchalance.

Many of these men, no longer able to find wealth in the turn of a shovel, sought to find it in the turn of a card. Gambling was epidemic, especially among those who could least afford it. Hunter, who had never played more than a gentleman's game of bridge, learned the rules and nuances of poker and soon found that his training in the ministry had taught him well the principles of winning at face cards—patience and discipline.

He also possessed something which could not be learned. The headmaster at the Princeton Theological Seminary where Hunter had studied once marveled that Hunter had the gift of discernment—the ability to read a man in his falsehoods. Whether it was a gift of the spirit or otherwise, the talent was invaluable for a gambler, and in the four years since he had left the ministry he had grown rich at the tables, satisfied by taking from the miners what they had scratched from the earth.

Hunter was a drifter, as all successful gamblers must be, staying in a camp only until the miners avoided his games or decided that he was cheating and threatened to lynch him. Hunter had worked his way south through Oregon, from the Rouge River valley down to San Francisco where he spent a full year getting rich at the tables and one day losing it all in a bank robbery.

That same month of his loss, word arrived that Spanish mines had been rediscovered in Arizona and silver flowed like the salmon in the Oregon rivers. He had seen too much to believe the stories of such finds, but he knew that there would be many who would. The men, not the metal, were the greater draw. Anyone so gullible as to believe wealth awaited him for the journey was just as likely to believe he could find it at a poker table. It was while passing south through Nevada on his way to Arizona that Hunter learned of the prosperous Goldstrike mining camp in the Utah desert and decided to test its gaming tables.

As Hunter entered Goldstrike he passed a man swinging by a noose from a large sycamore. He considered it an ill omen. That same day he began to plan his own exit, hoping to do so with as large an accumulation as possible to make the detour worthwhile. In gambling, Hunter religiously followed a simple stratagem: lose more hands than you win, but lose small and win large and let the winnings accumulate—for you can shear a sheep many times but you can only skin it once. After three months in Goldstrike he decided to make his kill—wool, blood, and bone—and get out of town as quickly as possible. The vigilantes had only hastened his inevitable departure.

※

Hunter took inventory of the provisions Isabel had packed. It was mostly buffalo pemmican and hardtack and he realized that she had provided enough for herself as well as him. It pained him to think of his refusal of her after what she had done for him. Except for the need for water, he could ride more than a week on the provisions. Water was always the problem. He had only half a canteen left and no way of knowing the availability of water on the ride south through central Utah. It was cruel land he was entering, punctuated with long white fields of alkali and littered with animal bones. Many had died for want of water in these parts, their tongues black and swollen with thirst: the desert's retribution for crossing it unprepared. Still, the Gosiute survived in this range. He would need to find their source of water by nightfall.

He mounted his horse and continued to ride the line of the Oquirrh range into the desolate Bingham basin. By midday his water was gone and he rode beneath a naked sun fervently wishing for the clouds and their rain. He sucked on a small stone to keep his mouth moist. As the sun started its welcome descent behind the range, he came to a place where a strong westerly wind assaulted the mountain with unusual velocity, shaking the trees with a rush like the sound of waves breaking across a sand beach.

High above him, on a rock terrace nearly obscured by a line of cedar, he spied something swaying in the wind: bulrushes, their heads peering over the side of a granite shelf. He ran the horse up to the ledge, tied its reins to a tree, and scaled the rock to the plateau where a spring gushed forth from the mountainside. Crawling on his stomach to the edge of the creekbed, he cupped his hand and tasted the water. It was sweet and clear, and Hunter submerged his face until he had to come up for breath. He drank until his stomach was full then lay back on the smooth stone ledge like a great lizard and closed his eyes, content to listen to the water's babble over that of his mind.

After a few minutes, he rolled over and climbed down from the rock then led his horse to a lower, marshy place where it could reach the stream. While the horse drank, he scouted the area for a place to camp.

He could find no cave or rock outcroppings in the area, but the sky was clear, so he staked out a flat parcel of land and gathered wood: gnarled deadwood for a fire and pine boughs for a pad on which to bed down beneath the open sky. Then he took his rifle down the mountain and within the hour shot a black-tailed hare. He was not particular; he was simply glad for fresh meat as he carried it back to his camp.

He started a fire with flint and stone and wood shavings, piling successively larger tinder until the fire blazed in a great flame. He set about preparing the hare, pushing its intestines down with his fist until they ruptured the soft belly. He skinned the animal, scraped the entrails with the blade of his knife, then speared the carcass on a wooden skewer and improvised a spit to roast his dinner.

His time in the West had taught him the ways of survival. He had eaten things, often under the compulsion of starvation, that he never would have considered in his previous life: from dog to raccoon.

As the meat cooked, the juices rolled off and

hissed in the flames, and he thought that he would have liked one of Isabel's corn biscuits with his meal. He thought again on the young woman and how pleasant her company had been. A verse from Genesis flashed across his mind. *It is not good for man to be alone.* He wondered if the walls that protected his heart were finally thinning and what else might go should they fall. He decided that he was just lonely. It is easy to think of jumping off a cliff into a lake, as he had seen the Mexicans do, until fifty feet of heaven are between you and the water's surface.

Grasping both ends of the skewer, he took the hare from the fire and tore the succulent meat from it with his teeth. It tasted better than he had expected. He congratulated himself on finding such a camp and considered that he might just stay awhile and live off the land as a mountain man. He had encountered frontiersmen in his travels, clad in fringed buckskin with winter hats made from the full, skinned carcass of coyote or fox, their lives spent in self-imposed exile. He had wondered, as all men do, if such an existence were a part of him. But the more he thought on it, the less appealing it seemed. "Hunter" was a family name and had nothing to do with warrior impulses. At least not his. Though he did not now look it, he was more a product of civilization than wilderness and he would rather negotiate a meal with his tongue than his hands. As good an orator as he was, he had yet to talk an elk out of its venison.

As night fell, he dragged a log across his fire and let it blaze as he looked up at the constellations and found the bears of Ursa Major and Minor, and Pegasus, and the arrow of Sagittarius. He remembered when he held her beneath the celestial blanket. Things were different then. The stars were different then. They were not a million angry eyes of God staring down at him. It was his last thought as he fell asleep.

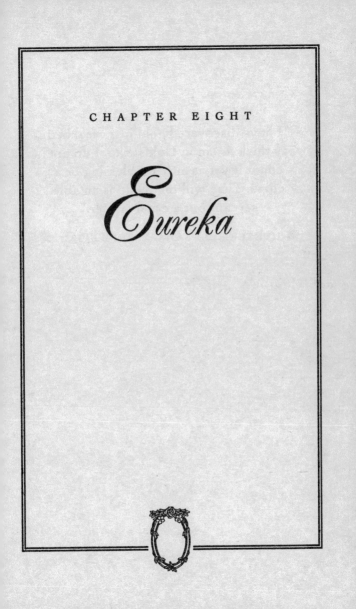

CHAPTER EIGHT

Eureka

"I have discovered gold in a creekbed as thick as sin in Goldstrike. I do not count it yet as either a blessing or a curse. Time will tell. Gold is an able servant but a cruel master."

❋ HUNTER BELL'S DIARY, JUNE 6, 1857 ❋

*H*unter woke early, hoping to cover enough ground by noon to stop for a siesta and to avoid riding in the hotter part of the day. He returned to the creek and drank his fill, then immersed his water pouch, canteen, and everything else he carried that would hold water. He knew that he had been fortunate in finding the spring, but such luck rarely struck twice. He might have to ride two or three days until he came upon another water hole or the next settlement.

As he completed filling the last of his receptacles, he noticed something he hadn't seen in the dim of the previous twilight: the submerged earth near the creek's bank was speckled with yellow flakes. He reached in and brought up a dripping handful of the flecked black mud. The pale yellow stones had the appearance of gold. For a moment his heart raced, then he smiled at his gullibility. There was simply too much to be gold. He had often spent days coaxing a thimbleful of metal from a ton of gravel and here the yellow ore was scattered everywhere, as if spilled from a jeweler's pouch.

He pinched one of the larger nuggets and held it up between his thumb and forefinger to examine it more closely. Then he gathered two smooth stones from the creek, lay the nugget on the flatter of the two, and pounded it with the other. To his surprise the yellow stone flattened with his strikes. He set his hat upside down like a bowl and dropped the gold inside. Then he reached back into the creek with both hands and scooped up more of the mud, bringing up even larger nuggets. He took his knife and began cutting into the earth. That same hour he brought up the largest nugget he had seen since he had come west—whether from his own diggings or on a poker table. He guessed it at twenty ounces or more.

He worked at the creek all day and did not stop to eat, his appetite for food displaced by his hunger for gold. By evening he had filled the felt hat halfway to the brim with pure gold. As night fell, he started a fire and ate strips of jerky and bland hardtack for dinner but did not begrudge it. It was only then that he noticed the strain on his back and shoulders.

For the next two days, Hunter dug with hands

and knife, bringing up the gold-laced soil by the handful. He wished for a pan or shovel, or any of the mining implements he had abandoned in his flight, but the pickings were so rich that he did not complain. Like hunting bear in a cage, he thought. He decided that he was losing too much gold sifting the silt between his fingers, so he poured the gold from his hat into his buckskin poke. Then he cut the top off of his hat and discarded its brim, using the hat's dome with some efficiency as a pan.

By midmorning of the fourth day Hunter had filled the pouch and an empty whiskey bottle with gold and there seemed to be no end to the metal. He mocked himself for his frenzied pace of digging. The gold had been there for millennia and wasn't likely to be going anywhere soon. The thing to do was to file a claim, get the proper tools, and go about this efficiently. Outside of Goldstrike, the next closest assayer's office was in the Great Salt Lake City. It was a day-and-a-half ride out.

Hunter cut his initials into the bark of a piñon, then paced thirty steps due east. He dug a hole and cached a portion of his gold in the event that he was stopped on his journey by Indians or bandits. The rest he would carry on his person or in his saddle-bags. He walked off a section of the mountain around his creek, gathering stones as large as he could carry to a pile that supported a large branch of scrub oak. He built such a mound at each corner of his claim.

He saddled his horse, then rode a ways off and surveyed the land, memorizing the particular peaks and markings of the mountain backdrop. Western lore was replete with accounts of lost gold mines. Though he knew many of the tales to be apocryphal, they were not all so and he had met miners who had spent their lives in pursuit of something they had only once seen.

As he looked out over the land he suddenly shouted out as if to an invisible congregation, "I proclaim this Belltown." His voice, carried on hissing desert winds, echoed back from the foothills and he glanced around the desolate, forsaken wilderness and recanted. "No," he said softly. "This must be God's neighborhood. I will call it Bethel."

He set out across the west desert toward Salt Lake City.

CHAPTER NINE

The
Great
Salt
Lake City

"I made the day-and-a-half ride from Bethel to the Great Salt Lake City, then made a spectacle of myself by loading down a wagon with enough supplies to keep until the Second Coming. I was noticed by all and no doubt I will be joined by a few prospectors after my return to Bethel. As sure as success will destroy a man, it will just as assuredly be imitated."

HUNTER BELL'S DIARY, JUNE 9, 1857

The Salt Lake City of the mid-nineteenth century was called The Great Salt Lake City, a bustling western town of more than nine thousand residents. Its inhabitants were mostly Mormon Zionists led west by Brigham Young and the soldiers that Congress had sent to keep an eye on them. Though it had taken the Mormon pioneers more than a hundred days to reach the valley from Missouri, seventy-five by handcart, there had been much progress on the trails since their arrival and a stagecoach with strong horses and a determined driver could now make the journey in just two weeks. The city was a regular stop now, as well as a destination, for those headed west. With the influx of western immigrants, a thriving business district sprang up in the city with banks and hotels, furniture stores, liveries, restaurants, saloons, and dry goods.

Hunter had camped the night in the desert and it was just before noon when he entered the city. Although he had heard tales of the Great Salt Lake City and its peculiar inhabitants, it was larger and more civilized than he had been led to believe.

He was tired and hungry from the ride. Stopping at the first restaurant he passed he ordered a loaf of bread, a pickle, and a beer. He discreetly brought his purse from his coat and paid the charge with gold. The proprietor of the restaurant stared enviously at his bulging poke.

"Fair 'mount of metal you got there."

Hunter looked at the man warily, but did not reply as he sat down at a table. He tore apart the loaf and wolfed down large chunks of the bread as the man watched him.

"Where 'bouts you be digging?" the man asked.

"West," Hunter replied tersely. When he finished the last crust he chased it with the beer then wiped his mouth with the arm of his shirt. "Which way is it to the assayer's?"

"Just east of us. There's a sign on the door."

Hunter nodded. As he left the restaurant he caught eye of his own reflection in the pane of a large glass window. He stopped and stared at his image. He looked as rugged as any man he had seen in the West and found it amusing that he'd likely frighten his parishioners if they saw him. As he walked away, he thought even more peculiar than his change of appearance was that after all the miles and years he considered his former parishioners at all.

Registering the claim was not difficult. There had been no claims staked within ten miles of Bethel, as it was considered a good-for-nothing wasteland uninhabitable by anything but a "digger-Indian." Hunter claimed twenty acres around the creek, drawing a map of the ground's lay from memory. When he had finished the paperwork he rolled the deed into his pocket then set about accumulating the provisions he had come for.

His first stop was the livery he had passed on his way into town. Parked for sale in front of the shop was a large Owensboro freight wagon that had made the journey west. After Hunter had climbed over and under it and determined it sturdy, he instructed the proprietor to fill the back of it with hay as he went and inspected the livestock. He selected two mules and a guernsey, then added three shoat pigs, a dozen leghorn hens, and a leghorn cock, as he had a taste for fresh pork and white-shelled eggs.

He paid the livery owner, hitched the mules to the front of the wagon, tethered his horse and cow to the back, and stowed the pigs and chickens inside in two wooden crates. Though he did not wish to draw attention to himself, as he had in the restaurant, he thought it unlikely that he could remain inconspicuous in such a task. He rode his caravan, clucking, grunting, and braying, off to his next stop, leaving the livery owner a pleased and wealthier man who immediately spread word of his good fortune.

Hunter distributed his gold to the proprietors of several more emporiums as he liberally loaded down the wagon with whatever provisions he thought he might require.

He started with food, purchasing large sacks of flour, wheat, corn, onions, and potatoes. Two ten-pound bags of walnuts in shells. Four one-hundred-pound sacks of beans. Tin cans filled with beef broth and stock. Cornmeal. Jerky, molasses and yeast, and a barrel of honey. Coffee beans and tea, pickled eggs, salt pork and beef. A crate of dried apples and several jars of canned fruit. Oil and butter. Malt, white wine and cider vinegar, and mixed pickles. Six dark jugs of whiskey.

At the dry goods store he procured a stack of heavy wool blankets, two of them of Indian weave. A canvas tent. A rain barrel. A box of nails. Several cast-iron skillets and kettles, a coffee grinder, and a Loysel's hydrostatic coffee urn. A rocking chair. A quill pen with ink. A cabinet and chest of drawers.

He bought a hatchet and lumber saw, two panes of glass which he wrapped in one of the blankets, and hardware for a swinging door as he intended to build a cabin upon his return.

He secured mining equipment: shovels and washing pans, a gold cradle, and a Long Tom and riffle box, several picks, an ax, an adze, and a box of dynamite. He bought two guns—a double-barreled shotgun and a single-shot cavalry rifle—two boxes of ammunition, and a pistol with floral etchings wrapping around its barrel just because he admired the way it balanced in his hand.

He purchased a new beaver-felt hat nearly identical to the one he had used as a gold pan, along with two flannel shirts and two pairs of denim jeans. Then, for reasons he could not recall later, he bought another hat—a bowler with a narrow rim.

He completed his purchases with gold still remaining in his pouch. Then he stopped at a restaurant and ordered the first fancy food he had tasted since San Francisco—oysters on the half shell and cauliflower cream soup—but he did not finish the meal. His taste had grown simple for the likes of corn bread, jerky, and beans. He considered only briefly spending the night in a hotel, with a porcelain bath and a barber's shave, before deciding against it. In this he realized more had changed than his appearance. He was no longer adapting to the culture of the West, he had become it. Only two hours before sundown, he climbed aboard the buckboard of his weighted-down wagon and began the trek back to Bethel.

CHAPTER TEN

Sonny Chang

"The miners have crashed upon my town like a wave from the great ocean of humanity. How quickly it is forgotten that Midas's gift was a curse, not a blessing."

❈ HUNTER BELL'S DIARY, JUNE 29, 1857 ❈

$\mathcal{C}$oncealing a sizable find of gold in the West was like hiding carrion on the plains of Death Valley—the vultures circle the hapless animal before it has even taken its last breath. Even before Hunter made it back to his camp, word of the Bethel find had made its way to the pages of the Salt Lake City newspapers. It was a sensational story, the kind folktales were born of—a mysterious man emerging from the desert with a sizable poke of gold. In local talk the details of Hunter's visit were embellished until he had supposedly bought out half the businesses in Salt Lake City with a find rivaled only by the Eureka.

Within a month, more than sixteen hundred men had descended on the foothills of Bethel town, oftentimes pitching tents and staking claims with the same sun. A main street was established, first with canvas tents, then with more permanent structures as cut lumber from the Salt Lake City mills was hauled into the town and sold at a premium. The first completed structure was the Bethel boardinghouse and it was filled to capacity even before its sign was hung.

The first of the miners to arrive in Bethel came from Salt Lake City and the neighboring towns of Provo, Ogden, and American Fork. Then prospectors began arriving from the bordering states of Nevada, Idaho, Wyoming, and Colorado. They were mostly white men, tramp miners and drifters, though peppered with the same races that filled all gold camps of the West: Mexican, Chilean, Negro—slave and free, and the Chinese.

Most unusual were the Chinese. While most miners came to Bethel solitary, their burros and gold lust their only companions, the Chinese came in parade, jostled in crowded wagons with paper lanterns swinging at the carts' hooped entrances, or on foot, shouldering their belongings on the ends of bamboo poles. They walked beneath broad-rimmed hats woven of split bamboo, their braided queues falling to their waists, their strides accompanied by the slap-slap of wooden-soled slippers.

The Chinese immigrants were a familiar part of the western landscape as more than a hundred thousand Chinese had already immigrated to America. As one newspaper editor tersely reported, they were "as plentiful as rats in a junk's steerage." Still they were a peculiar enough sight to induce a man to lay down his shovel and watch them pass.

❊

The Chang family had sailed in 1853 from Nanking province with the largest wave of Chinese immigrants. They had landed in San Francisco, hunted for gold east of the city, and over the next four years panned and picked their way northward toward Sacramento. It was there that word of the Bethel discovery reached them, circulated and sensationalized throughout the West by newspapermen hoping to rid their communities of immigrants. The Chang family left California in hopes of richer and more hospitable soil in Utah and, upon their arrival, staked claim of the bed down creek from Hunter Bell's. It took only one day for the family to construct a small compound of tents and brush houses.

Hunter was surprised that the Chinese had claimed ground so close to his own as they rarely took up any claim other miners would think worthwhile to work. Had they happened to strike a rich find, they almost certainly would have been driven off their claim by the white miners.

Oftentimes they would wait until the whites had

abandoned a worked-out claim then move in, using their more sophisticated measures to harvest the passed-over gold from the site. They were from a different world, an older and more patient one, methodical, and often ingenious. In one camp, a group of Chinese purchased a worked-over claim and shack for twenty-five dollars from a group of white prospectors who mocked the Asians as they left with their money. The Chinese immediately set to work at prying loose the floorboards of the shack and recovered more than six hundred dollars in gold dust that had fallen between the cracks in the floor. Their ingenuity did not impress the white miners and the group was found the next week hanging by their queues, their throats slit.

Hunter was not mining the week the Chinese settled in. He had already cached a fortune—more than fifty thousand dollars of gold—and having settled on a lay of ground that overlooked his claim, he was now seeing to the more practical matter of building his cabin. It was a task that proved nearly impossible for a lone man. He was growing doubtful of the enterprise when the Chinese arrived. Three days after their arrival, he approached them to see if they were willing to hire out.

As he emerged from a cedar and piñon thicket into the sloping lay of their camp he stopped to observe their curious workings. A few of the men carried implements of which he had never seen the likes before. The Chinese had skill from their previous life of flooding rice paddies and knew methods unknown to the white prospectors in how to divert a stream from its course, so that its rich bed could be accessed and mined. The small company had already begun the construction of a dam.

There were a dozen people in all, including four women and a child, a wide-faced boy of five. Most were dressed similarly in loose baggy pants and heavy knee stockings and except for one elderly woman, the women worked alongside the men and carried as much of the physical labor.

As Hunter advanced, he was noticed by the small boy, who was playing on the bank of the creek. The child hollered and the group stopped working and each man gazed anxiously upon the intruder. One of the Chinese, a slight man who appeared younger than the other adults and was the only one wearing denim and flannel, lay down his shovel and timidly approached Hunter. The other men also lay down their tools. A woman retrieved the child and carried him back to a tent where the other women had gathered.

Hunter had not interacted much with the Chinese. In his travels he found that they kept to themselves—rarely entering the saloons or joining in the poker games. It was not that they did not indulge in games of chance, as they gambled incessantly in vociferous sessions of mah-jongg, but they played among themselves and more for entertainment than gold.

The young man approached to within a few yards and removed his hat. He was flanked by the other men, all nearly a head shorter than Hunter.

Hunter crossed his arms at his chest. "My name is Hunter Bell. My claim is upstream of yours." He pointed to the east end of their diggings. The men looked at him quizzically and Hunter wondered if any of them spoke English. The eldest man said something in Chinese to which the slight man replied. He walked forward, pulled a paper from his sash, and held it in his outstretched arms. Hunter glanced at the note.

> *Notice is hereby given that we the undersigned claim three hundred feet of this bar and bed of the river for mining purposes in 1857 and 1858.*
>
> CHANG YAN & CO

"I did not come to contest your claim. I came to see if you would be willing to help me build my cabin. I will pay you for your service."

There was no response.

"Build cabin," Hunter repeated loudly, pointing toward one of their brush houses.

The emissary turned and spoke again in Chinese. After staring at Hunter for a moment the elder nodded his head. The young man said with a thick accent, "You pay us. We help you build."

"You speak English, then."

"I speak a little."

"What is your name?"

"My name is Chang Jya Lung. My America name is Sonny."

Hunter put out his hand. "My name is Hunter Bell."

The man cautiously accepted his hand.

"How are your diggings?"

"Not good," he said quickly. Hunter could have predicted the response. The Chinese would never lay claim to success, not for reasons of humility, but for survival.

"How much money do you want?"

He turned back to the elder. *"Dwo syau?"* he asked in Mandarin.

"Shr wu kwai chyan."

"Fifteen dollar."

Hunter frowned and rubbed his chin. "That is a lot to pay for a day's labor."

"To build the cabin," he replied.

Hunter said, "Then you are not paid enough. I will pay you twenty-five dollars."

The man looked at him curiously then turned to the other men and spoke. Their anxious countenances eased. The women and the child came out of the tents.

"What did you say?" Hunter asked.

"I tell them you honorable man."

Hunter did not acknowledge the tribute. "When can you assist me?"

"We come now."

To his surprise, the entire group abandoned their work and followed him back to his site. Sonny translated as Hunter showed them where he had been cutting timber and had begun strapping the pine poles to his mules and dragging them one by one to the site. The males spoke among themselves; then three men and all the women went to work stripping the fir logs while the boy sat quietly nearby, amusing himself with an anthill he had discovered. The rest of the men set to cutting down more trees. They constructed a simple cart with wheels made by sawing off sections of the larger logs and cutting a hole inside for the axle. The group hauled the large logs down to the site until the logs accumulated below in a large jam.

The next morning Hunter was awakened by the sound of the Chinese shouting in their sharp tongue. Even before the sun had made its full entrance, the group had gathered to work and a disagreement had arisen on how to proceed. Sonny was sent to Hunter to explain the dilemma. They were troubled with the lay of Hunter's cabin. Sonny explained the necessity of *feng shui*—to build the cabin in accordance with the surrounding landscape and nature. They wanted to place the cabin door opposite of Hunter's instructions, facing away from the mountain, as there was a wall of harsh rocks sure to carry destructive energy. There was also a rock that had the appearance of a sinister head which they believed contained a particularly malevolent spirit. While Hunter did not take such things seriously, the Chinese demonstrated such concern that Hunter sincerely doubted their intention to proceed and acquiesced to their desires.

It took two days for them to stack the walls and a day and a half for the roof, which they erected with a grade that pitched in harmony with the mountain's slope.

Hunter took advantage of the supplies being imported by Bethel's growing number of merchants and more than once drove the wagon into town for additional supplies. He purchased planks of milled lumber and wooden pins and built a puncheon floor. The last addition to the cabin was a swinging door which Hunter built using the hinges he had purchased in Salt Lake City. He was pleased at the ease with which his door swung. The Chinese likewise acted impressed and each took a turn opening and closing the door.

When they had completed the cabin, Hunter negotiated with the Chinese to continue on in his employ. They cleared a grove of cedar pines, leaving standing a circle of the trees to which they horizontally lashed the fallen pine to make a corral. Then they built a stable for the livestock and a privy.

They finished on the eve of the sixth day (an irony not lost on the preacher), and as the night fell, Hunter stood back, looked at his new home, and pronounced it complete. He slept that night on the floor of his cabin. The next day, at Hunter's invitation, the Chinese returned. Hunter slaughtered one of his pigs and the women prepared and roasted it and they feasted together. He paid them forty dollars in gold—twenty-five for the house and an additional fifteen dollars for their work on his stable and fence—then made them presents of his tent, a large jug of whiskey, and a barrel of sugar. Hunter shook each of their hands, accompanied with a slight bow, a ritual which now was becoming habit to him. Sonny handed him a scrawled receipt for his payment, which amused Hunter, and which out of politeness he did not discard.

Before returning to their camp, they hung above his door a red banner inscribed with Chinese characters in black paint, which Sonny translated to read: "Wealth, happiness, and long life." Then they lit a string of firecrackers that echoed loudly throughout the foothills.

"What is the meaning of the firecrackers?" Hunter asked.

"To frighten away demon spirits."

"It will take a might more than gunpowder to accomplish that," Hunter said sardonically.

The cabin was large for just one man. It had one window, which was about three feet across and glass paned. It had a stone-and-brick fireplace with a simple pine mantel on which balanced the whole of Hunter's dinnerware: two plates, a tin cup, and a stein. With lumber left over from the floor, Hunter constructed a short porch outside the front door with a pine rail and a bench, then a sawbuck table and another bench and a shelf next to the fireplace which he planned to fill with books.

It had been years since Hunter had had his own place, outside of a canvas tent, and he found himself desirous of adding every convenience available. The finished cabin was sparsely furnished. He sewed his own curtains and nailed them over the windows. In Bethel he purchased a five-foot oak pantry with a built-in flour bin, a thick mattress of twill ticking stuffed with meadow grasses, and a buffalo hide. He constructed a simple bed frame from arm-thick pine poles; he planned to carve the poles into fancy spindles during the confinement of the winter months.

It was not until a week later that he was finally satisfied with his lodgings and he returned to the creek and began to bring up its gold.

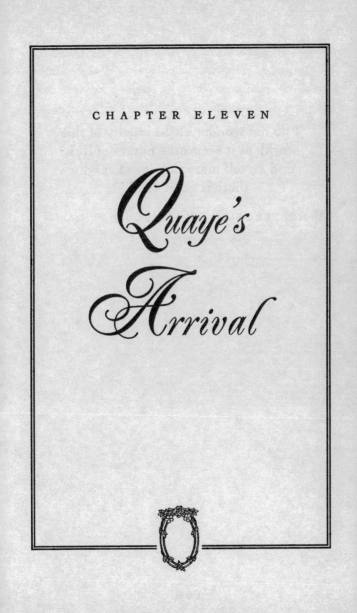

CHAPTER ELEVEN

Quaye's

Arrival

"I do not wonder at the cruelty of this world, as it seems the nature of it. I find myself more perplexed at why there is good at all."

❁ HUNTER BELL'S DIARY, AUGUST 19, 1857 ❁

*O*n the sweltering late-July day that Quaye arrived in Bethel she did not take much note of the camp, as it was not unlike any other western town she had seen in the last six years.

She rode on the back of her husband's horse, her head cloaked in a cabriolet bonnet. The bonnet, once considered a status symbol in her native land, was worn at Jak's insistence. It covered the bruises that marked the sides of her face from the previous night's beating and other beatings still too recent to have faded. She no longer counted the marks. The deeper wounds were not manifest on her flesh.

But if Quaye did not take notice of Bethel, the town took notice of her and the arrival of a woman in camp caused no small sensation among the miners. In the West female society was said to be rarer than an honest lawyer. In one gold camp completely bereft of women, miners had lined up and paid a full dollar just to look on a woman's corset. Ironically, the brutal West demanded better treatment of women than the East and Jak had learned to not hit Quaye in public lest there be retribution. Like most who prey on the weak, Jak was a coward.

Jak reined the horse at the boardinghouse, told Quaye to get down, then climbed down himself. They were met inside by the boardinghouse owner. Quaye stood behind Jak, her head slightly bowed. The owner was no taller than Quaye, bald, with a long beard as if the hair had slipped from the top of his head to the bottom. He wore a red flannel shirt and Levi Strauss trousers held up by suspenders. As he watched them enter, it took him great discipline to not stare at the young woman.

"We need boardin' for two," Jak said.

"Sorry, but I ain't got any rooms left. Already got men sleepin' on the dinin' room floor." He gestured to a cluster of bedrolls as proof. "I suggest ya purchase yourself a tent. They got plenty of 'em next door at the mercantile."

Jak frowned. "Do ya need a woman to cook and clean?"

The man looked at Quaye. "Could always use a woman's hand."

Jak recognized the familiar look of desire in the man's eyes. "What will ya pay?"

"Dollar fifty a day. And victuals for the lady."

Jak knew the monetary value of his wife. "Ya can have her for two dollars and a half. And we both eat."

The man rubbed his beard. "Two dollars. And ya both eat."

Jak looked hesitant and the man added, "And ya can make a room in the barn. Ain't no animal in it anymore since my horse died."

"We spent our money gettin' here," Jak said.

The man reached into his pocket and brought out some bills. "I'll advance ya two days' wages if she'll start next mornin'."

Jak pocketed the money. "What hour?"

"A half hour before sunup."

"She'll be here."

As the two of them left, Jak grumbled about the stinginess of the proprietor while Quaye remained silent. She was glad for the job. Anything to take her away.

"I'm needin' a drink," Jak said. "You go water the horse then see about our place."

"I am hungry," she said.

He handed her a twenty-five-cent piece. "When ya have seen to the horse, ya can buy yourself some bread."

Quaye took the coin, then grabbed the horse's reins and did as she was told.

CHAPTER TWELVE

Jak Morse

"Is man good and bent evil by society, or is he born evil, and kept straight by society's heavy hand? Most disturbing to me about this question is not its answer, but the reason for which it is most often invoked."

❊ HUNTER BELL'S DIARY, AUGUST 19, 1857 ❊

*J*ak Morse was born to a poor family in a small shack an hour's walk from Macon, Georgia, though neither the town nor state would be proud of that. The locals that remembered Jak's father, Lucius Morse, all said that he was a superstitious man prone to violent outbursts, usually directed at Jak and his mother. He believed Jak was born under a bad moon and had pronounced to all the kinfolk present at the boy's christening that the one-month-old infant would amount to nothing. It was probably to Jak's benefit that Lucius disappeared before Jak turned six, though it would be hard to imagine that the boy could have turned out much worse.

Jak's mother, Virgie Morse, was a rigid, religious woman who claimed her wealth was her faith and wore her suffering proudly as a sign of piety. She never once sought to protect herself or Jak from her husband's violence, as she attributed all misfortune to God's will and, as God chastens those he loves, gloried in the fact that she must assuredly be one of God's elect daughters.

She did not spend much time with Jak, except to discipline him, which she did with great severity and at the slightest impropriety. Not surprisingly, Jak grew mean. Blind to her own contribution to his disposition, she often wondered if perhaps there was something to what her absent husband had said about the boy—if it were possible that a child might just be born bad.

Jak was not yet eighteen when his mother took ill with the consumption and was bedridden. Jak felt no compulsion to care for his ailing mother and one morning, with the chickens unfed and tomatoes ripe on the vine, he left to make his way in a different world.

After walking west for a fortnight, begging food and sleeping in haylofts, he found employment as an assistant to the plantation overseer. It was a position well-suited to his temperament. The slaves soon learned to fear him, for he was as sadistic as he was lazy and he drove them as inhumanely as any overseer ever had.

He prospered in the position for nearly six months until he took a fancy to one of the slaves, a young girl of ten who helped in the kitchen. He attempted to force himself on the frightened girl and was caught by the cook, a large black woman called Miss Linnie who ran the house with a Bible in one hand and a skillet in the other. Jak was no match for the woman. She soundly thrashed him and scratched his face up until he fled, bleeding and humiliated. An hour later he came back with a gun and shot her.

While he did not have to answer to the laws of the land for the murder, the laws of the plantation were a different matter. The Seddons, the plantation owners, were partial to the woman; particularly Mrs. Seddon, who favored Miss Linnie's company and cooking. Mr. Seddon, who was now out his investment in a valuable slave, saw that Jak was tied to a tree and flogged until he could barely drag himself from the property.

As Jak recovered he decided to seek his fortune at sea. He hiked north to the New York waterfront hoping to find work on a seagoing ship. Instead he found employment exploiting the hordes of famine Irish arriving daily in the American ports.

The Irish, whose only desire at the end of their dreadful voyage was to disembark and find shelter in the new land, were scarcely prepared for what they would encounter at the end of their long journey. Once the ships were securely docked, men swarmed over the bulwarks onto the decks: grasping, unctuous men who spoke with a feigned brogue.

These ruffians were employed by the taverns and boardinghouses to lure the overwhelmed immigrants to the establishments where most of their remaining cash would be efficiently extorted from them. In addition to the commissions they earned, the "runners" charged exorbitant rates for their services and were backed up by thugs both for protection and coercion should a weary family try to resist. Jak had no fear of the law in this employment, for the local magistrate's only concern for the Irish was to keep them from begging on the streets or picking New Yorkers' pockets.

It did not take Jak long to master the routine. He would climb onto the ship with the other men, eye a family, and seize onto their bags. "Don't ye worry yerselves, ole Jak's got ye bags. An Irish family, God bless ye! Ye be in luck today. I've just the place for ya, a safe dwelling, mind ye, in this frightful city. A place where ye can ponder and decide yer future with good will and Irish smiles to share."

After a half year on the job, Jak learned there were still greater profits to be made from the Irish in acting as a broker—selling passage on ships with delayed sailing dates or that were in need of repair. He sailed to Ireland and that which he did to the

Irish in the New York ports he did more profitably to them in Cork. After he sold passages to the ship, adding two shillings to the cost of every pound of sea stock, he drove his client emigrants to establishments where board and bunk would be available at exorbitant rates until the ships were ready to sail. The hapless country folk were lodged in the filthiest of circumstances, the sick ar.d the well together, several to a room, for three pence a night all paid in advance.

The average stay in Cork before sailing was a week to ten days and the runners and lodginghouse keepers made the most of the time hawking all sorts of "necessities" to the credulous emigrants: camp beds, fishing tackle, and water cans, and food that barely deserved the appellation—cans of used tea, rancid flour, and sugar laced with sand.

Jak found that the desperate circumstance of the Irish made them exceptionally vulnerable and the last week of his stay on the island he began a new ruse, selling month-out passage on a vessel that did not exist.

He was engaged in such fraud when Connall McGandley had happened upon him. It was unfortunate for Quaye that Jak had not abandoned her on the New York dock as he had planned. Quaye was young and vulnerable and Jak was one willing to make her pay for being so. In a world that chewed up Jak and his ilk, it was as if he had taken a prisoner from the other side.

On the voyage back to America he made her ride in the steerage, except for when he desired her, until she caught dysentery and was no longer allowed above deck.

Jak soon learned that Quaye was a commodity that, if properly exploited, could ensure his livelihood and drink. America was not a kind place to the Irish, which further assured Jak's control of the frightened young woman. He employed whatever means necessary to guarantee that she would remain his beast of burden. Between her frequent beatings, he reminded her that she owed him her life, as miserable as that life might be, and even though she had come to hope that he would take it from her, she also believed him. At least after years of his abuse she began to believe some of it.

Quaye had learned to close herself down to the beatings, to watch her body thrashed like it were some inanimate object without life or heart. But beatings alone did not satisfy Jak's sadism and so he would contrive tortures to break her spirit, tormenting her with her desires until one by one she lost all hope for happiness.

In spring of 1851, nearly four years after Quaye's arrival in America, Jak dragged her to the California coast. She proved even more valuable in the West than she had in the East. Jak had as little success in prospecting as he had in any other endeavor, but if his dream of easy wealth had vanished, his life of ease hadn't, as the burden simply shifted from the riverbeds to Quaye.

❊

Quaye did not object to her new surroundings. Though the stable still carried the stench of its former inhabitants, its roof and walls were solid and come winter would provide better insulation than a tent. The boardinghouse owner had brought out a small cot, which was claimed by Jak, while Quaye slept on a blanket laid over hay in one of the stalls or over the remnant tasseled husks in a corncrib, both of which were preferable to Jak's side. She was accustomed to working long hours and was glad to be gone during the day when Jak was home and home at night when he was gone. He was rarely around her when he had money to drink or gamble, unless he woke her in the night with groping hands, his breath reeking of whiskey.

While Jak gambled or drank away most of what she earned, Quaye rose at four each morning and stoked the coals in the barn's rude firebox then walked in the pre-dawn darkness to the boardinghouse and began preparation of the miners' breakfasts and box lunches. When she finished serving, she would deliver lunch to Jak then return to clean the kitchen and house and prepare the night's meal for the boarders.

Quaye was liked by the miners, though she kept her distance; she knew the penalty if Jak caught her speaking to one of the men. But even if Jak had allowed her to freely socialize, she would not likely have done so. Life had taught her to fear men.

The miners gave her occasional tips, which she politely acknowledged then put away in an empty baking soda canister discarded from the kitchen. She doubted Jak would let her keep the money, but she fantasized that she might be allowed a portion of it and someday hoard enough to purchase herself a store-bought dress. She held to the dream until one night she came in and found Jak sitting on his cot holding a half-empty bottle of applejack in one hand and a silver coin in the other, his face glowing with drink and rage. The tin canister was at his feet, its contents spilled on the strawed floor.

"What is this?" he asked in a low, guttural voice.

She spoke timidly. "It is money I put away."

His eyes shone with the glint that had grown familiar to her and she knew that it was too late to alter the course of events. He stepped toward her. "You are stealing from me?"

She dared not look at him. "A miner gave me extra. I was going to tell you . . ."

"Tell me?" He shoved her into the corner of the barn. She grabbed her shoulder where she had collided with a wooden timber. "And what did ya give'm in return?"

She brushed her hair back from her face. "He was pleased with my cooking."

He raised his fist and she instinctively cowered. "What else did you give him?"

"Nothing. I'm sorry. I shouldn't have kept the money from you."

She covered her face with her hands. He cuffed her ear, grabbed her by her hair, and pulled her head forward then slammed it back into the wall. He began to hit her, not in a reckless flurry of fists, but slowly and deliberately, as she futilely tried to cover herself. While she plead for forgiveness.

"I'm sorry. I won't do it again. I won't steal from you again."

Jak continued to hit her until he found no more satisfaction in it. He turned and went back to his drink. Quaye slumped down into the corner of the room. She softly whimpered and did not even touch the blood that rolled down her chin. She did not cry loudly, for he would beat her for that too. She had learned her world's rules for survival.

CHAPTER THIRTEEN

The *Woman* in the *Snow*

"It is silent now, the blizzard has paused and left the moment still. I think about them both at such times — roaming the shadowlands of memory amidst the shards of my broken heart."

❋ HUNTER BELL'S DIARY, DECEMBER 8, 1857 ❋

*B*ethel's first snow came in mid-October in a whisper that dusted the ground and did not hamper the mining activity in the camp, though fires were kept and the miners began their winter preparations in earnest, stockpiling food and firewood and patching holes in tents and cabins. Three weeks later the first snowfall of substance came, measuring more than six inches. The work in the lode mines continued, as the temperature did not change much in the bowels of the earth, but Bethel was mostly a camp of placer diggings. The surface ground was soon too frozen to even pick at and both the creek and the miners' activity froze to a trickle.

It was the time of hibernation, when the miners would gather in their shelters, staying inside for weeks at a time, playing cards and talking, mending equipment, but mostly just devising means of staying warm. Most miserable were those who lived in the tents or in earth-walled shelters dug into the mountainside, who spent their nights in disrupted stretches of sleep, wrapped in blankets and feeding fires, and their days congregated in the saloon for warmth.

On the sixth of December a blizzard hit the mountain, relentlessly fueled by gale-force winds that dropped temperatures to fifty below. The winds howled incessantly, shrill and ghostly through the mountain like the discordant moanings of a thousand specters.

Hunter's cabin was high on the mountain. For three days the winds drove the snows around him, piling drifts against the west wall of his cabin until the snow provided an unbroken slope from the snow-covered ground to the pinnacle of his pitched log roof. Inside, Hunter waited it out. He drank and slept in turn and read everything he owned twice. He tossed cards or practiced his sleight of hand, shuffling decks of cards and making cards disappear and reappear—tricks he never used at the gaming table, but could with little fear of discovery. He had started the task of carving the bedposts, taking the bark off of the poles and whittling away the edges to create a balled cap. He considered turning it into an artichoke before he grew weary of the task and lay his knife aside.

It was shortly after midnight of the third day when there was a break in the storm's fury and the fierce winds paused, breathless from the onslaught which left the foothills entombed beneath a shroud of white.

Hunter was awakened by the sudden calm. He lay in bed staring into darkness, testing the potency of his insomnia. After about an hour he conceded to it, lit the kerosene lantern by his bed, then crossed the room to pile wood onto the glowing embers of the dying fire. If he had had a clock he would have known and perhaps cared that it was nearly a half past two, but his timepiece had not been wound since he left San Francisco. A clock was a habit of a more structured world alien to his.

He took up a kettle and went to the cabin door but found that he was sealed inside; the snow had frozen at the threshold and piled against it. He heaved his shoulder into the door and pushed it open. He was met by the rush of cold air that braced his skin. He lingered at the threshold, looking out over the pristine landscape. The clouds had broken, parted beneath the moon which reflected brightly off the crystalline blanket. It was never dark on winter nights until the moon set.

He scooped the powdery snow into the black iron kettle until it rose above its rim. Closing the door, he returned to the hearth. He placed the pot on the fireplace armature and swung it over the flame, then he filled his coffee urn with grounds. When the water in the kettle bubbled, he poured it into the urn's funnel until it had filtered to the top of the urn, filling the room with the aroma of the coffee. He re-covered the urn and poured himself a cup out of the tap. It was dark and strong. It was a rare extravagance, as he had grown accustomed to the miners' coffee, a gravy of a brew percolated in a coffeepot half full of grounds.

He sat in the rocker next to the hearth to listen to the silence. He did not often choose to leave such moments sober, as a quiet mind was a precarious thing. But he was in no mind to drink so he went to his bureau and brought out his diary—a leather-bound journal cracked with age—a quill pen, and a vial of ink. It was a custom that had endured from his previous life. He learned that by some strange wizardry of transcription, he could, in the process of recording his thoughts, distance himself from them—as if to confine them by ink to paper. In keeping with the physicality of ritual, he preferred the more tedious quill to the ease of a fountain pen. He dipped his pen in a bottle of ink and began to write.

It is silent now, the blizzard has paused and left the moment still. I think about them both at such

times — roaming the shadowlands of memory amidst
the shards of my broken heart. I fear less the hell
that must assuredly await me in the beyond than
that which is born of my own life and its remem-
brances. I have considered that they are, perhaps,
the same — that Hell is nothing more than a clear
recognition of what we are and what we might have
been. . . .

He lifted his pen in thought and gazed into the
fire, mesmerized by its lapping tongues of flame.
Suddenly the night's tranquility was broken by the
voracious snarls of wolves. Hunter set aside his
journal. It was likely that the blizzard had driven
wolves from the higher elevations down to the
foothills to feed on the miners' livestock.

He pulled on his boots and his heavy coat, then
grabbed his rifle, inspecting its bolt as he stepped
out into the thigh-deep snow. It had snowed more
than three and a half feet and he trudged around to
the back of his cabin with great difficulty.

About sixty paces from the cabin, close to the
stable, he spied three timber wolves: swift dark
shadows plowing through the powder in a dance of
conquest. They had brought something down and
the animal nearest him, its teeth bared, tugged at
the prey while the other two pranced about their
kill — a small black heap barely visible above the

snow. Hunter raised his rifle and fired. A wolf barked with the slug then fell writhing next to its prey. The gun's recoil echoed through the mountain and the wolf's companions retreated momentarily to the cover of the foliage, staring with gleaming amber eyes as Hunter approached.

To Hunter's surprise the fallen animal was still alive though it moved sluggishly as one dying. Not willing to let an animal suffer, Hunter lifted his rifle and cocked back its hammer as he high-stepped forward. He stopped and let his rifle fall.

It was not an animal but a woman lying unconscious in the trampled snow. She was small, likely a Gosiute squaw, he thought. Hunter cautiously moved closer, jammed his rifle butt down in the snow, then squatted next to the woman. The surrounding snow appeared black with her blood. She was not a squaw, but a white woman, her pale skin red with cold. She wore no coat and her feet were bare, her shoes likely lost in her flight from the wolves.

Suddenly a wolf charged from the darkness. Hunter grabbed his gun and swung as it lunged at him, striking the animal and falling backward in the same motion. As the animal returned he leaned forward with the rifle and fired. The slug threw up a patch of hair and the wolf yelped and tumbled forward into the snow, then retreated into the blackness.

Hunter tucked his rifle under his arm and knelt in the snow over the woman. Cradling her in his arms, he lifted her, then swaggered backward, his gaze fixed on the black shadows that followed his retreat.

When they were back inside the cabin, he lay the woman across his bed, then turned up the wick on the lantern. She was shivering. Her mouth was open and her teeth chattered between her moans. He brushed the snow from her body.

Blood was dried and caked above her lip and the side of her face was badly bruised. He thought the pattern of the marks peculiar; they were not congregated in one angle as if she had fallen, but were random, as if she had been struck repeatedly. Her shoulder was a mass of blood and a flap of skin was laid back where the wolf had torn her flesh. The wound would need to be attended to, but at the moment it was frostbite, not the lacerations, that concerned him. He had encountered men who had been caught crossing the plains by early snows and lost extremities to frostbite: noses, ears, fingers, toes, and even limbs. He continued his examination down her body. Her hands and arms were red with frost, but not ashen. Her ankle was bent an unusual degree; it was likely broken, but the discoloration of the skin of her feet gave him greater trepidation.

He went to the fireplace, emptied his coffee cup

against the firewall of the hearth, then dipped the cup in the pot of water. Finding the water too hot, he grabbed some of the snow that had fallen inside the doorway, stirred it into the cup with his fingers, and returned to her side. He slowly poured the water over her feet, gently rubbing them as he did so, as the water soaked into the mattress. He thought it fortunate that she was unconscious as she would likely have to be restrained if she were not. He repeated the process, then went to his cabinet and brought out turpentine and castor oil, set them near the bed, and began massaging her feet with the spirits. When the turpentine had evaporated, he rubbed her feet in castor oil, then removed his wool socks from his own feet and pulled them over hers.

He noticed that her shivering intensified and he began to fear hypothermia. He retrieved the woolen blanket from the chair near the fire and brought it to the bed. He split her wet dress with his knife, leaving her in a chemise, and swaddled her in the heated blanket, then piled two other blankets on top of her. He pulled her bleeding arm from beneath the covers. The flesh would need to be sewn.

He retrieved a needle and thread from his cupboard. He was not unfamiliar with a needle nor clumsy with it, as he had of necessity darned his own clothing for nearly four years. Flesh would be easier to sew than buckskin. He poked the needle through her skin, stitching it crossways as well as he could. Her moaning increased. He tied off the stitches then cut the thread loose with his knife. He poured whiskey over the ragged wound, then wrapped her arm in a flannel cloth. It turned deep crimson.

She suddenly began to flail, trying to throw the blankets from her body. He fell across her, pinning her to the bed. It is a strange paradox of hypothermia that those suffering with it, their bodies dying from chill, attempt to strip their clothing, as if to speed the process.

Though he was much larger than she, the woman was strong for her size and it took nearly all of his strength to hold the blankets in place. They struggled this way for several minutes when the violent motion abruptly stopped and the woman's limbs froze rigid. Her breathing was now almost imperceptible and her face was ashen. Her arms turned a grotesque blue, as her body fought to survive by shunting its blood flow from the body's extremities to its core.

Hunter knew that she did not have much time left. Her body had lost the ability to heat itself and if her temperature did not soon rise she would go into shock and her heart would stop. He tore off his shirt and climbed into the bed with her, pulling her chill body into himself and pulling the blanket tightly around them and over their heads to create a tent. His heart raced in fear and he spoke to the unconscious woman, pleading with her as he pulled her into himself. "Keep with me," he said. "Keep with me. Don't let her die, God. . . ."

It was a slip of his tongue and the words echoed back at him with the frightening realization that he had been here before—pleading with God, his body pressed against the cold, damp skin of a dying woman, her skin ashen as wax. As if the nightmares that God had sent to haunt his sleep were not enough, God had sent to him the very thing he had run from the night that *she*, God, and his heart had died.

The realization filled him with equal rage and terror. Hunter wanted to run from this as well, to throw this strange woman back outside and let the wolves take her. What was she to him? Let her blood be on the beasts. His heart blackened at the vengeful God who had come before His time to torment him.

He spoke aloud, "I will not give you the satisfaction. There will not be another lost at my hands." He pressed tighter against her, then he put his mouth over hers and breathed into her, filling her lungs with warm air. He had counted twenty-three breaths when she again began to shiver and he continued until he could feel the skin beneath him gradually warm—until the shivering body that had been incapable of holding the heat it drew from him began to warm itself.

The lantern had gone out, leaving the cabin lit by the dancing illumination of a dying fire. He did not reckon how long it was before the blush returned to her extremities and the shivering ceased, replaced by the serene rise and fall of her chest. Nor did he notice the tears that pooled in the corners of her eyes and fell down her cheeks.

An hour before dawn, Hunter rolled off of her and lay exhausted on the mattress. This time he had beaten God.

CHAPTER FOURTEEN

The *Stranger*

"By some conspiracy of Heaven or Hell (I know not which), a woman has been placed in my keeping. I am reminded of the proverb: A strange woman is a narrow pit."

❈ HUNTER BELL'S DIARY, DECEMBER 9, 1857 ❈

In the darkness and frenzy of the night, Hunter had not noticed that the woman in his bed was beautiful. She was still sleeping when he woke. A single shard of the noonday sun broke through the partially veiled window as he sat up in bed and looked at her.

The curves of her face were graceful and feminine with pronounced, high cheeks and fawnlike eyes. Her lips, once again red, were full, yet sharp as if cut with a sculptor's knife. Despite the bruises, her face was unlike the haggard, leathery faces of the women most prevalent in the territories; rather she reminded him of one of the fresh, pale-skinned young women from the East that he would encounter from time to time—unfortunate females dragged from good homes by gullible, gold-lusting husbands who had read too many accounts of easy wealth.

She was not as voluptuous as the dance girls who attended the card games in the hurdy-gurdy houses in San Francisco, but had a pleasant, though slight, figure. Her long, auburn hair was matted with blood and dirt and lay tousled beneath her like a net. Her dress, lying on the floor at the side of the bed, was homemade, but this was not immediately apparent, as it was skillfully tailored and patterned after the habiliments he remembered worn by the more urbane women in his former parish.

The fire had died while they slept, leaving the room chill and dark. He rose from the bed and pulled back the curtain over the window, then set a new log with kindling in the andirons, blowing the embers until they glowed white-orange and burst into flame. When the fire was sure, he took the rocking chair from the hearth and brought it to the side of the bed and sat. He leaned forward and touched her forehead with his palm. She was warm now with fever.

As he gazed at her, he wondered whether she had indeed been sent by God to torment him or if her presence was merely a peculiar hand of fate. Hunter's land was well removed from the town's thoroughfare, sequestered by acres of cedar and piñon, and the townspeople kept their distance. Even in summer, few approached his cabin. Why, in a howling blizzard, had she trespassed his claim?

As he looked at her, the woman sighed and her head fell to one side. Her eyes fluttered, then slowly opened. She looked at him then glanced down at the torn dress crumpled on the floor, then back at him. As their eyes met she pulled the blanket up to her chin. He felt accused by her stare.

"Your dress was wet. You nearly caught your death of the chill."

She did not speak, but gazed at him guardedly.

"I don't have any snakeroot for your fever," he said. "If it does not soon fade I'll boil cottonseed. I suspect you hurt all over." After a moment of silence he said, "I had best examine your limb."

Though apprehension was still evident in her eyes, he crouched by the side of the bed and pulled the blanket up around her leg. Gently peeling down the stockings, he found the flesh of her feet was pink and recovered of the frost. Her left ankle was, as he remembered, bent at a peculiar angle. He gently stroked her leg until he felt where the bone was irregular then moved her ankle slightly; she tensed but did not cry out and he thought she held a high tolerance to pain.

"You have broken your ankle," he said. "It needs to be set."

He left her side and returned with two narrow

slats of wood, frayed strips of cloth, and a wide-mouthed bottle containing comfrey leaves mixed with snow. He again crouched by her side.

"I am sorry, but this will hurt some." He gently pulled on her ankle, testing its rigidity, then in one swift motion he jerked it into alignment. There was an audible snap and she gasped slightly. Her face paled and showed her pain but she made no sound. He packed the snow and comfrey leaves around her ankle. Positioning the small planks by her side he began binding the cloth tightly around her leg.

"I suppose you might say the wolves were a blessing. I would not have known you were outside my door if it wasn't for their howls." He finished tying the cords then stood. "It will be a few days before you can walk on that. I don't know how you came to be outside in the blizzard without a cloak." After a moment more of silence he said, "You must be hungry. I'll bring you something to eat."

He left his chair and went to his pantry. He heaped a bowl full of oats, filled it with water from the kettle, and allowed it to steep a minute before he stirred it and brought it to her. "I made you oatmeal."

She made no move toward it and so he set it on the floor by the bed. While Hunter was accustomed to the silence of his own life, he was not so accustomed to it in the company of others, especially female company. He spoke to break the tension. "I reckon you'll eat when you're hungry." He put his hands in his pockets. "Well, I've got chores." He walked to the door, pulled on his coat and boots, then went outside.

Hunter did not return until late that afternoon. He furtively glanced at the woman as he stepped into the cabin, his arms cradling a bundle of fire-wood, but she did not look his way and he dropped the load in a pile next to the hearth. He pounded a log against the wall to break off its clinging ice, then placed it, hissing and smoking, onto the fire.

"How do you feel?"

She still did not speak. He walked over to her. She had tucked the dress beneath the covers next to her, and the food by her bed had been touched but was not gone. She lay on her back with her arms above the blanket. He noticed that the wrap-pings on her arm had loosened. He deduced that she had removed the bandage to inspect the wound for herself.

"What have you done here?" He reached over her to inspect the bandage and as he lifted his arm above her, she flinched. Hunter stopped. He stepped away from her.

"You need not fear me. I would not harm you." He moved farther back from the bed, his gaze still fixed on the silent woman. She lifted her hand to her matted hair and tried unsuccessfully to run her fingers back through the mud-caked strands. "There is earth in your hair. If you like I will bathe it."

She expressed no opposition, audible or otherwise, so he went and put warm water into a small tin washbasin. Then, covering the base of her neck with a rag, he gently propped her head with a pillow. He took the water up in a cup and poured it first over her crown, then to each side of her head. He let the warm water seep into her hair and then he followed it with a rag, running it through to her scalp, gently stripping out the mud and grass. He wrung the cloth until the water in the basin turned umber with blood and mud.

It was an intimate act, and she closed her eyes as he washed her. When he finished, he gently patted her hair, then he wiped dry her forehead and neck.

"I'll get you something to wear." He returned with a flannel shirt which he lay across the bed; it would drape on her like a gown. "On the morrow I will bring you something more substantial than oatmeal. Something with some venison in it. Meat will do you good."

He wondered if the woman was unable to speak, then decided that he had said enough to compensate for her silence. "I'll leave you now. There's a chamber pot at the foot of the bed."

He had just turned when she spoke.

"Why didn't you let me die?"

Hunter turned back and gazed at her before he answered. "Well, ma'am, I leave the business of killing to God."

The woman just blinked at his response. Hunter tipped his head. "Good night, ma'am."

He went off to the far corner of the room.

CHAPTER FIFTEEN

The

Preacher's

Soul

"There are those who deny the
existence of God and there are those
who have witnessed too much to deny
the unseen world, and deny
themselves of the love of God. In this I
am the most hopeless of men. For
there is not much hope to be found in
hating a God, if you believe in Him.
And there is not much future in it."

❄ HUNTER BELL'S DIARY, DECEMBER 10, 1857 ❄

$\mathcal{T}$he woman's voice stayed with Hunter and her peculiar question replayed in his mind. Her voice had been timid and feminine, tinged with an accent of indeterminate origin. He thought that it sounded somewhat like a brogue, if only the remnant of a past tongue.

Hunter had laid out his bedroll amid gunnysacks of beans and barley in the corner of the cabin. The dawn had not yet woken when he emerged from his woolen blanket, went to the hearth, and stoked the fire. In its flickering light he looked back at the woman. As far as he could tell she was still asleep, as she lay facing away from him.

He commenced to making breakfast. Quaye woke to the sizzling of great slabs of bacon and she first mistook the sound of it for rain. The pungent aroma of coffee and bacon filled the cabin. She watched him as he delivered a platter of bacon and eggs fried in drippings, setting the food on the floor next to her bed. He proceeded silently, as if he were entertaining the new trust of a bird he did not wish to frighten off. Their eyes met briefly. She said, "You're the preacher."

"Is that how I am known?"

She nodded. "Much is said about you. In the town."

"What is said?"

She held her tongue and Hunter sensed that she was fearful of sharing what she had heard. "It is all right to say what you hear."

"They say you sold your soul to the devil."

Though Hunter smiled in amusement the woman looked anxious still. ". . . Some say you're a murderer."

"A murderer?"

"A man at the boardinghouse claims to have known you in Pennsylvania. He told all in the dining room that you killed your wife and came west to escape hanging."

The smile left Hunter's face. But though the accusation clearly affected him, he made no effort to refute it. She wished that she had not shared the slander.

"I am from Pennsylvania," he affirmed. He sat down in the rocking chair, then said thoughtfully, "I reckon the first appellation is more correct."

"You were a preacher?"

"A lifetime ago. A life ago." After a moment he asked, "What is your name?"

"Quaye."

"Quaye," he repeated, feeling the word in his mouth. "A peculiar name."

"It is Irish."

"What were you doing out in that storm?"

Quaye's face tightened and Hunter wondered what shame could be had in being caught in a storm. "There is a band on your finger. Your husband will be anxious. Later today I will ride into town and let him know of your whereabouts. Where will I find him?"

"I suspect you will find him at the saloon."

"At the saloon?"

"He plays cards."

"I would think that he would be out looking for you."

She shook her head. "He put me out in the storm."

Hunter cocked his head as if he did not understand her reply.

She spoke mechanically, as if recounting an event in which she had no part. "Jak was drinking hard. He was angry for being holed up. But then he ran out of whiskey. He ordered me out to get more, but I wouldn't go because of the blizzard. When I refused, he beat me, then he threw me out into the snow without my cloak. He would not open the door to me. I told him that if he would give me my cloak I would go beg him some whiskey, but he wouldn't. Every place I went was barred against the storm, and the winds were too loud to be heard over. I was so cold." She lowered her eyes and her voice fell. "So I started for the mountain."

"Why the mountain?"

"I didn't want to be found in the public square."

Hunter sat back in the chair and rubbed his chin. He had not reckoned on such an explanation and was not sure of what to say. He finally said, "My name is Hunter."

"If I may stay just one more day. I will be grateful."

"You won't be going anywhere for a while," Hunter said. "Not until your ankle heals. Unless you want to be crippled for life."

"I must be back to Jak."

Her insistence on returning to the man who had almost killed her perplexed him. "You are not a prisoner here. But it would be best that you stay awhile."

She considered her predicament. She did not know if Jak was sufficiently drunk to have forgotten the events of the night, but he would be angry at her for breaking her ankle and would make her work regardless. Even though a beating was certain on her return, she would be best off to let her ankle heal.

"I need mend my dress," she said.

Hunter pushed himself up from his knees. "I do not have enough thread in the house to mend your dress. And your boots are lost. When the weather allows, I will purchase what you need in town."

Her face fell at the news of her boots. Two years previously, Quaye had lived an entire year without shoes until she had been gifted boots by a rancher's wife she had met in Vacaville. "My boots are lost?"

"I suspect they are buried in the snow. I will buy you new ones."

She feared what he would require in compensation. "I have no means to repay you."

"I do not require repayment," Hunter said.

As he returned to his corner of the room, Quaye wondered exactly what manner of man he was.

CHAPTER SIXTEEN

Syau Lou

"I have learned a great truth of life. We do not succeed in spite of our challenges and difficulties, but rather, precisely because of them."

❀ HUNTER BELL'S DIARY, DECEMBER 13, 1857 ❀

The next two days passed mostly in silence and stretched long into the night, as neither Quaye nor Hunter slept well. Sunday's afternoon visit was a welcome respite from the quiet. Sonny Chang had come, accompanied by the five-year-old boy Syau Lou. The boy's mother, Hwa, stood behind him, her arms draped over his shoulders and clasped at his chest, holding him next to her. Hunter invited them in.

Quaye watched them enter with great interest. Though she, like Hunter, had encountered Chinese in the West, she had never spoken to one and thought them as peculiar as anything she had found in the new land.

"Hwa want boy to be American," Sonny said.

Hunter wondered what it had to do with him. "Was he born in America?"

"Yes."

"Then he is American."

"She want you teach her son read English."

Hunter glanced at the boy and his countenance revealed a strange, deep pain.

"He is too young," he finally said.

"He learn now and he not speak English like Chinese. We pay you."

Though Hunter owed a debt of gratitude to the Chinese, he could not bring himself to accept. The boy's mother gazed at him hopefully.

"You teach him," he said to Sonny.

"I cannot write but few words."

"Who wrote your claim? I read that."

"I copy it from San Francisco *huiguan.*"

Hunter shook his head. "I'm sorry. I just can't."

When Sonny saw that he had made up his mind, he bowed. "I sorry trouble you, Mister Bell." With his head still stooped he began to walk backward.

Quaye spoke up. "I will teach him."

Sonny looked up quizzically; he had not realized that someone else was in the room. For the first time he saw Quaye.

"Your wife?" he asked.

"She is not my wife."

"Ah," Sonny said, nodding knowingly.

"It is not that way," Hunter said.

Quaye looked at Hunter. "If you will allow it, I will teach the boy."

"What can be learned in but a few weeks?"

"I can teach him every day. After I go he can come to the boardinghouse. I will teach him there."

Sonny glanced back and forth between the two. Though Hunter's face revealed his displeasure with the offer he finally said, "She will teach the boy."

Sonny asked, "What hour you teach?"

She looked at Hunter for approval. "Tomorrow noon," she ventured.

"Jung wu," Sonny said. The boy's mother smiled.

"Sye, sye. Sye, sye," she said, repeatedly bowing as if the room were crowded with people. After they left, neither Quaye nor Hunter spoke to each other.

❊

Syau Lou arrived the next day precisely at noon. He brought a knapsack which contained paper and a Chinese hair-brush pen with a bottle of black ink, and a gift for his teacher, a large glass jar of black tea.

Quaye did not leave the bed, but she leaned over its side while the boy sat on the chair next to her. She began the lessons by writing out the whole of the alphabet on a sheet of his paper and made him repeat it over and over, practicing each letter's sound. The first lesson went on for three hours. Hunter sat at his table cleaning a gun for the first hour, then left the cabin. He looked in on them several times and did not return until the boy was gone. That night he asked her if she planned to keep all the lessons at such length. She replied that with his permission she would. Hunter went out to the stable and returned with a flat-end hatchet and a coil of rope. He pounded a nail slightly above the height of his head into the wall, bent the nail over, tied the rope to it, then crossed the room, pounded another nail, and secured the opposite end of the rope. He took several blankets and hung them over the line, partitioning Quaye and the bed from the rest of the room.

"Now you don't need to worry about your privacy."

It did not surprise her that he seemed inconvenienced. He had lived in solitude or in the presence of men and now shared his cabin with a woman and a child. She suspected his annoyance had less to do with her than the presence of Syau Lou, and was surprised by this, as he clearly liked the Chang family. She decided that he simply did not like children and left it at that.

Quaye took pride in her young pupil. Syau Lou learned quickly and after the first week she could point to any letter on her alphabet page and he could pronounce it. He had also learned how to say her name, as he found it close to Chinese and easy to pronounce. Quaye relished each moment she spent with the child and the maternal feelings evoked by the little boy's presence. Quaye had never conceived with Jak. And as much as this saddened her, she also believed it a blessing from God.

With the curtain in place, Hunter no longer left the cabin during the lessons. Ironically, though he had seemed to disapprove of the sessions, Hunter was intensely interested in them and, as they went on, would often inquire as to the boy's progress. And he would always smile at the child, though there was a peculiar sadness in his eyes.

She suspected that Hunter had listened in on their lessons but it was no more evident than on Christmas Day. Quaye had asked Hunter for an old stocking which she filled with some walnuts and a candy stick. She told Syau Lou the Christmas story, then presented him with the gift. After the boy left, Hunter was quiet and sat staring at the fire. Quaye asked him if he was all right. All he said to her was, "I didn't know it was Christmas."

❄

The day after, as Quaye concluded the day's lesson, Sonny burst into the room. His eyes were wide with excitement.

"Mister Bell!"

Hunter set aside his book. "What is it, Sonny?"

"Men come say we must leave today. They say claim belong to them."

"What men?"

"White men. They take our claim paper and go to town with Lau Jung. They say they have miners' council for white men only." He looked at Hunter, hoping to find an ally against the council. Hunter wondered why the men would jump a claim in the middle of winter. "What started this?"

"Lau Jung went to town to buy lamp oil. Bad men see his gold and follow him back to our camp. They tell us we must leave now or they shoot us every one. We show them our claim but they say it not right and they take it from us. They take Lau Jung away. Say we take him when our wagon leave town or he hang tonight."

"How many men were there?"

"Six men."

Hunter frowned. "I will see what I can do," he said.

Sonny spoke sharply toward the curtain, "Syau Lou! *Ni ma shang hwei jya, ba!*" The boy quickly emerged from the partition, retrieved his coat, and scurried out of the cabin. Quaye had heard the conversation but sat quietly behind the curtain as Hunter strapped a Colt revolver to his hip and walked out. Quaye worried about what would happen to him.

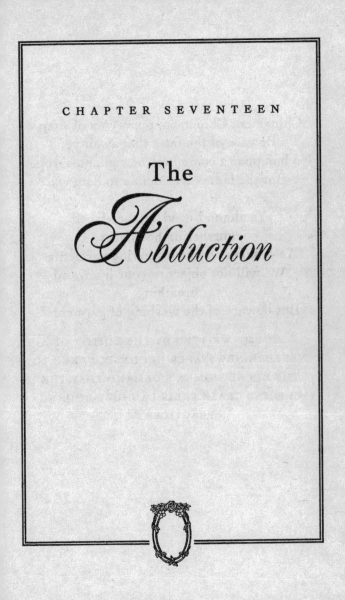

CHAPTER SEVENTEEN

The
Abduction

Chinamen, Chinamen, purveyors of soap,
   Beware of the fates that await ye;
No hangman's committee or vigilantes' rope,
   But the ladies are coming to hate ye;

    Ye almond-eyed, leather-faced
       murthering heathens!
   Ye opium and musk stinking varments,
   We will not object to your livin' and
       breathin'
   But beware of the washing of garments!

✳ RHYME WRITTEN BY THE EDITOR OF A
WESTERN NEWSPAPER IN CONSEQUENCE TO
THE LOCAL WOMEN'S DEMAND THAT THE
CHINESE CEASE THEIR LAUNDRY-BOILING
PRACTICES ✳

ord of America's gold was brought to China by enterprising ship owners who foresaw potential profits in Chinese mass emigration. They distributed bulletins along the coastal towns of China, extolling the gold-laden soil of California where a man could set his tent stake and pull up enough yellow metal to retire a gentleman. They called California *Jin Shan:* Gold Mountain.

The Chinese immigrants were initially welcomed and flowed into the new land by the tens of thousands. But as California's stores of gold diminished, embittered prospectors, struggling for the most meager subsistence, found the Chinese a visible and plentiful target on whom to vent their frustration. Public opinion turned on them. Newspapers and politicians alike advocated measures for expelling them—denouncing them as heathens, opium addicts, and looters of sluice boxes who were a threat to everything holy in a land where nothing was. The Chinese, once appreciated for taking the jobs no one wanted, were now hated for it. They were regarded as nothing short of a curse—a faceless, nameless mass of humanity that swept over the western landscape like a great yellow scourge.

Without the protection of society, groups of white robbers preyed solely on the defenseless Chinese, stealing their gold, their land, and their lives if they resisted. Of such atrocities one newspaper editor wrote that he "didn't mind hearing of a Chinaman being killed now and then," then kindly admonished his readers not to kill them "unless they deserve it," but when they did—"why kill 'em lots."

❊

As the two men rode into town, Sonny pointed out the men's horses tied outside the saloon. At the saloon's entrance Hunter motioned to Sonny to stay outside the door.

In one corner of the bar the men had congregated around Lau Jung, who was bound to a chair, his torso bare and his hands tied behind his back. His nose was bleeding, as he had been struck repeatedly. There had been a wager as to whether or not they could make a Chinaman's nose still flatter. A stout, red-faced man with thinning hair held something that resembled a horse's tail and was trying to force it into Lau Jung's mouth. Hunter realized that it was Lau Jung's queue. The whole of the saloon's occupants were entertained by the Chinaman's plight and goaded the men on with the abuse.

A passage from Ecclesiastes flashed through Hunter's mind. *They gaped upon me with their mouths, as a ravenous and roaring lion . . .*

He rested his hand on his gun. "Untie him."

The occupants of the bar turned nearly in unison and it was evident from some of their faces that at least part of what Quaye had spoken of him was true—they feared him. When no one moved to release the man, Hunter stepped forward and pulled his bowie knife from his belt and cut the ropes himself. Lau Jung rose unsteadily. Hunter took his arm and escorted him from the circle of men. No one made a move to stop him.

"Stay away from my claim," Hunter said.

The man holding the queue scowled. "A Chinaman's claim ain't worth the yeller flesh that penned it."

"It's not their claim. It's mine. I bought it from them last autumn." Hunter produced the receipt that Sonny had written him for their building of his cabin and held it up. "I have a receipt of sale right here. Does anyone challenge it?"

One of the men shouted, "Why them Johnnies camped up there?"

"They work for me."

While a Chinaman's claim was considered fair game, stealing land from a white man was an altogether different matter. The men, now condemned by the whole of the miners, all backed down. All except for the red-faced man who was still on his feet. "Ain't no Johnny lickfinger gonna tell us what we gonna do. He's lyin'. I seen them Johnnies' gold myself. Ya'll yeller?"

Hunter glanced about coolly. Then one of the men said, "Leave it, Jak. It's been claimed."

Hunter guessed at the man's identity. "Jak Morse?"

The stranger looked perplexed. "What's it to you?"

"You are nothing to me," Hunter said. Then he spoke loud enough for all to hear. "I'll not only shoot any man who comes on my property but you trouble me on this and come spring I'll divert my creek. We'll see how you favor drywashing." With Lau Jung ahead of him, he walked toward the door, leaving the room silent behind him.

"Divert it where?" a miner asked after him.

"I'll flood the meadow for rice paddies. My Johnny friends have a taste for rice."

As they left the saloon, Lau Jung's shorn head hung in shame for the loss of his queue. Sonny did not speak and his expression showed his distress. "You take our claim?" he finally asked.

Hunter looked over at him, his face still grim from the encounter. "You listened in?"

Sonny nodded.

"It is the only way you will hold your land. You can have whatever you take from it," Hunter replied.

Sonny's face relaxed. "I understand," he said.

Before they left town, they stopped at the dry goods store where Hunter purchased thread, a pair of women's shoes, and, for the Chinese, four shotguns. Sonny felt the gun in his hands and caressed its shaft.

"Now we keep bad men away."

"Don't be thinking that you have any idea how to use that thing," Hunter said flatly. "I'm going to have to teach you to fire it. Then you'll need to practice."

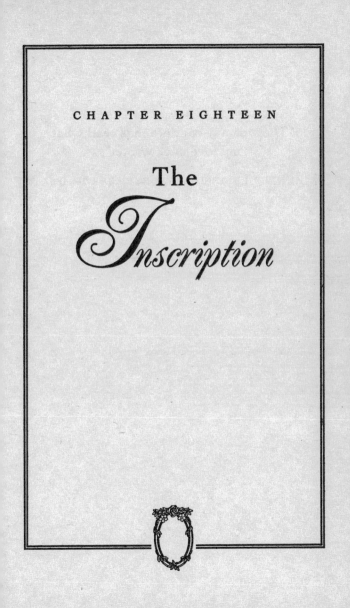

CHAPTER EIGHTEEN

The
Inscription

"The woman, Pandora, has read what
my love once wrote."

❈ HUNTER BELL'S DIARY, DECEMBER 26, 1857 ❈

*H*er first day in the cabin, Quaye had spied the fireplace shelf with its dusty volumes and wondered then if there was a Bible among them. Despite her faith, it had been more than seven years since she had held a Bible. Born Catholic, in her turbulent years she had looked to her religion for strength. At first Jak thought her faith foolish but benign, and though he mocked her beliefs, he did not object so long as it did not interfere with his demands. But as he saw that it began to restore what he had stripped from her, he took steps to remove it from her life. Her rosary beads were discarded. She was barred from attending mass or from taking communion, then from even speaking of her faith. Finally he would not allow a Bible in the house.

With Hunter gone, Quaye lifted her legs over the side of the bed. She took a single step and pain

shot up her leg. She grabbed onto the chair for support. She took a deep breath then again put pres-
sure on the ankle. She was not one to heed pain's
whining and had learned to distance herself from it.
She slowly hobbled across the room, arriving at the
other side breathless. She leaned against the shelf
as she looked through its volumes.

To her surprise, she could find no Bible. She had
mistaken Hunter's leather-bound diary for scripture, which she opened, then, realizing her error,
replaced on the shelf. She found a thin book of sonnets and leafed through it, then carried it back
across the room. The book showed the wear of
much reading; its spine was broken and its pages
discolored around the edges. She lay back in her
bed and opened the book. The flyleaf was inscribed
in beautiful calligraphy.

❋

My dearest Hunter,
If only my lips could use such words as my heart so
casually speaks — that the clouds of my mind
might not obscure the sun of my love. But I, of all
women, should be most content with my lot and
express in love's duty what my words strain to
share.

You are my light and one true dream. You are my

faith and my religion and I lay my heart at the altar of your love. How glad such submission!

Oh, dear husband, see how quietly my pen endeavors to speak what my soul wishes to shout. Thus I gift to you this book and borrow another's words and if my pen cannot claim ownership, my heart fears not to plagiarize . . .

"The face of all the world is changed, I think,/ Since first I heard the footsteps of thy soul . . ."

WITH ALL MY TENDER AFFECTIONS,
RACHEL

✳

The inscription filled her with curiosity. She wondered what man might elicit such devotion from a woman. Even more puzzling, if the sentiment expressed was honest, where was its author, leaving the man she loved alone? The thought called to mind the rumor of his wife's murder. Though Quaye doubted its truth, she could not explain his strange response when she spoke of it.

She passed over the page and began reading the sonnets, but after only a few pages she returned to the inscription and read it anew.

She found other mysteries within the book. Inserted between its pages was a daguerreotype of a small girl with large, dark eyes, her hair falling over her forehead and to her shoulders in sausage curls. Quaye thought her pretty and wondered her relation to the man. There was no inscription on the picture other than the scrawled *Philadelphia 1856* on the back, but next to the image were two letters: one folded and tucked beside it, the other in a sealed envelope, closed with sealing wax embossed with a gothic letter *B.* On its face was written *Hannah.* At first Quaye left the letters alone, until her curiosity became too powerful and she returned to them. She would not open the sealed envelope, but she carefully unfolded the brittle paper of the other.

❧

February twelfth, 1856

Pastor Bell,

I pray my epistle finds you well. Bless you for the sustenance you have most recently provided. You have always been of a generous heart. Hannah is well, in health and spirit. It is evident from the picture that our Lord has blessed her with her mother's beauty, as well as her father's great spirit, for both are bared in her countenance.

Many await and pray for your joyous return to our flock and to His fold. Until then, may God's peace follow you.

SISTER FOLLAND

❈

When Quaye heard the approach of Hunter's horse, she refolded the letter and tucked it back into the book, setting the volume on the far side of the bed. After a moment Hunter entered, set his gun on the table, then went and took a ladle of water from the rain barrel. As she watched him, she realized that the words of the letter and the inscription had affected her perspective. He looked different to her now, as if a portion of his exterior had been peeled back to reveal a new man.

"Are you thirsty?" he asked.

"Yes."

He ladled the water into a tin cup and brought it to her with the satchel containing his purchases. He handed her the cup.

"Did you find Lau Jung?"

Hunter nodded.

"What happened?"

"They backed down," he said softly.

Quaye gazed at him with admiration.

"Syau Lou will not be coming for the rest of the week," Hunter said. "His mother is frightened." He opened his satchel and brought out a cone spool with a needle stabbed into it. Then he extracted a pair of leather, ankle-high boots with a dozen eyelets for lacing. "I've brought your thread and boots. I suspect the boots will fit. They are not Adelaids."

"Thank you," she said demurely. "I did not expect Adelaids." As she caressed the boots Hunter spied the book lying next to her. His expression abruptly changed.

"What have you there?"

Quaye looked at the book then back to him. His expression frightened her. "Your book of poetry."

"Where did you get that?"

"I'm sorry, I didn't mean to pry. I was looking for a Bible. I did not think you would mind."

"I have no Bible," he said tersely. As he took a step toward her, she instinctively cowed, anticipating a blow, but he only reached over and took the book. For a moment he gazed at the frightened woman. Then, without a word, he carried the book back to the shelf.

CHAPTER NINETEEN

The
Burial

"A great tragedy has shadowed our world."

❊ HUNTER BELL'S DIARY, DECEMBER 28, 1857 ❊

he rest of the evening passed in tension. Hunter felt remorse for his display of anger and for his loss of Quaye's company. She had retreated back into her silent world, as she methodically repaired her dress in anticipation of her departure. He wished that Syau Lou would come, as his presence always made her happy.

The next morning, Hunter made her a breakfast of corn pone with honey and boiled barley tea, then, without a word, left the cabin. He returned several hours later with a heavy box. He set it on the bed next to Quaye without explanation, satisfied to leave it to her own discovery.

"What is it?" she asked.

"They are for you."

Quaye lifted the box's lid to expose a stack of books and her lips parted in an inaudible gasp. She lifted each book individually, running her fingers across their embossed leather covers. *Wuthering Heights, Paradise Lost, Moby-Dick,* and a new edition of the book of poetry *Sonnets from the Portuguese.* At the bottom of the stack lay a leather-bound Bible. She stared at the book as if it were a holy apparition. She remembered the time she came home to find her Bible gone and Jak's harsh warning about its presence in their flat. She had protested vehemently and had been beaten so severely that even Jak seemed to feel some remorse. It was the only time she could ever recall that he had asked her how she was. Quaye touched the Bible, gently opened its cover, and her eyes began to well with tears.

"I know you meant no wrong by looking through my book. I am sorry I frightened you. When you return you may take them with you." He hesitated, then said, "Perhaps there is a place you could keep them from Jak."

Quaye marveled that he understood. "They are wonderful," she said. "I could keep them at the boardinghouse." She laid them all out on the bed. "Have you read them all?"

He nodded. "I read about everything I can get. I left an extraordinary library back in West Chester."

"Is that where you are from? West Chester?"

"It is where we . . ." He redirected his reply. "It is where I preached," he said quietly. Quaye noticed that the slip had left him discomforted. She lifted *Wuthering Heights*. "I have heard of this book. I desired to read it. But I do not often have the luxury of books."

"That doesn't surprise me. I've met your Jak," he said.

The words chilled her. "Where?"

"At the saloon. He was one of Lau Jung's abductors. He was as loathsome as I imagined he might be." He noticed the fear now evident in her face and he said to reassure her, "He does not know that you are here."

Quaye turned back to the book. She had begun to read the first page when she heard several loud pops echo through the mountains. Quaye looked up. "Your Chinese friends are exploding firecrackers."

"No. I purchased them guns to protect themselves. But they should not . . ." He stopped midsentence and his forehead wrinkled, his demeanor turning as attentive as a deer catching the scent of a stalking puma. Quaye held still and listened, for what she did not know. Then she too heard it, a low rumbling that grew in intensity until it seemed as if the ground itself began to tremble. The kettle hanging over the fire began to sway.

"Is it an earthquake?" she asked in a hushed tone.

Still focused on the noise, Hunter shook his head. "Avalanche."

The noise continued to rise and he strained to judge its distance.

"Are we in its path?"

"I don't know. . . ." He paused. "No. It is north of us. Near the Chinese."

Hunter ran to the door and, pulling on his coat, disappeared outside.

❊

By the time Hunter arrived at the Changs' camp the avalanche had passed, cutting a swath through the forested mountainside, laying the trees flat and splintered on its slide to the base of the mountain. The slab of the avalanche had passed about a hundred yards north of the camp, though its flank had spilled outward, toppling the wagons and partially burying two of the tents in its wash. A mule at the north end of the camp was buried to its breast in snow and was braying loudly. The clan had already gathered outside their tents, surveying the devastation in complete disbelief of the innumerable perils this strange new land held.

"Are you all right?" Hunter shouted.

Sonny waved his rifle. "We are not killed, Mister Bell."

Just then one of the women began screaming. "Syau Lou! Syau Lou!"

Sonny's countenance changed. "Her little son is not here!"

The camp immediately fanned out across the fallen snow, with Hunter joining the search, high stepping through the thick bed left by the avalanche. Each passing minute seemed longer as the cries of the distraught mother echoed in the wilderness. More than fifteen minutes had passed before Hunter spotted a fleck of color protruding from the glistening surface. Hunter waded toward it, almost hip deep in the snow, then fell forward, frantically clawing with both hands at the ice around the child. He shouted out for help. By the time the others arrived the child's leg had been uncovered and the men all fell to their stomachs and dug. The mother wailed hysterically, attended by the other women who tried to comfort her.

Syau Lou was unconscious but still breathing, as he had fallen in such a way as to create a pocket of air around his head. But his lips and fingertips were blue and Hunter recognized the advanced progression of hypothermia. The men lifted the boy from the snow. Hunter wrapped the child in his coat, then, with the family in tow, carried him back to his cabin.

Hunter brought the child to the fireside. The

boy's mother stayed close to him, clinging to her child's arm. The rest of the group clustered around them, looking on helplessly. At the group's entrance Quaye had gotten up and stepped from behind the partition. When she saw Syau Lou's limp body she covered her mouth with her hand.

As he had with Quaye, Hunter cupped the child's mouth in his own and began filling the child's lungs with warm air, but the child did not warm and the little boy, already blue lipped, stiffened and a deep rattle came up from his throat. Hunter lay the child down, winded from his own effort, his head bowed with the child's mother. When he looked up, Quaye saw that his cheeks were streaked with tears. He asked Sonny, "How do you say I am sorry?"

Sonny lowered his head. *"Bau chyan,"* he replied somberly.

The mother wrung her hands as she rocked back and forth, her face twisted in anguish. Hunter bowed his head. *"Bau chyan. Bau chyan."*

The room's only sound was the fire's crackling and the mother's whimpering. The family soon left, the grief-stricken mother carrying the dead child against her body with her husband's arm around her. After their departure Hunter sat quietly by the fire with his head drooped over his knees.

"I should not have given them guns," he said.

Quaye limped over and sat near him. For a time neither spoke as the fire crackled and sputtered, devouring the cedar boughs. Quaye wiped back her own tears, then spoke. "On the voyage to America, most of us Irish were kept belowdecks. It was damp and rat infested. We were all sick, seasick, but there was cholera and dysentery and typhus.

"There was one woman whose wee child took ill just a week at sea, and got sicker with fever. The mother rocked her baby to comfort him, but he would only stop crying for the brief times he slept. I don't think his mother slept at all. After the second day I went to her and asked if I could hold her child, to let her sleep, but she just looked at me with desolate eyes. I knew that she knew it would not be much longer. When I awoke the next morn, her child was silent. During the night he had died in her arms. She still held the child and she still rocked him. She did not cry.

"Word of the child's death was passed above deck and the men opened the hatch and her child was taken. Because of our sickness, the woman was not allowed above. I held her hand as we heard them drop her son overboard. She wept then and I wept with her." Quaye turned and looked at Hunter. "I did not believe that I would ever meet a man such as you. You are good."

Hunter held his head with both hands. "You are mistaken. I abandoned my soul three thousand miles ago. Back with my life and my ministry."

"You have it still."

Hunter did not respond.

"What turns a man from the ministry?"

"Devil's alchemy."

"By what alchemy is gold turned to lead?"

Hunter looked down and did not answer. At length he sighed.

"About seven years ago I graduated from the Princeton Seminary. I had found favor among the elders of the church and they granted me a congregation outside of Philadelphia. It was a small congregation, but it was devout and well established. While serving there as pastor, I met a young woman named Rachel." He paused as he realized that he had not spoken the name aloud since he left West Chester. He felt as if he had opened a grave. "Rachel and I were married. After only a year, Rachel declared that she was with child. She desired a child so greatly. I desired whatever made her happy. To Rachel it was only a beginning. She wanted a large family. One that would fill a wagon. It was the time of our greatest joy." There was a distant look in his eyes, an expression that evolved from the fondness of recollection to the subsequent horror of reality.

"Nearly four weeks before expected, Rachel went into labor. It was in the middle of the night and the baby came quickly. We lived in the country. There was no time to go for the midwife. Then Rachel started to bleed. The bleeding wouldn't stop. I didn't know what to do. There was nothing I could do but pray. I had never prayed so fervently in my entire life. I promised God that I would give him anything he asked for, if he would spare her life." He looked down and his eyes were now wet. "As the blood drained from her body her skin turned ashen. Like wax. She complained of being cold as I held her. So cold. I tried to keep her warm. As the sun rose she died in my arms." He breathed in deeply and it was a while before he spoke again. "A few hours later one of the church sisters found us. She took the baby while I buried my heart in the cemetery next to the church. I went into the house and packed and never returned."

Quaye did not speak for a moment. "The little girl whose picture is in the book is your daughter?"

He looked up and his eyes were moist. "She is beautiful, isn't she?"

Quaye nodded.

"She's a little more than four years of age, now."

Quaye touched his arm. Hunter had never shared this part of himself with anyone. He could not explain why he shared it now, or with this woman, but he could not keep it from her. He had no desire to keep it from her. "God took everything from me that night."

"And so you are angry at God?"

"I suppose that my anger is more of habit now than sentiment."

"I am sorry," she said tenderly. The two sat quietly for a few more minutes before Quaye leaned over and kissed him on the cheek then limped back to her bed.

CHAPTER TWENTY

The Funeral

"I have learned much about loss from their pain. Oftentimes it takes the darkness of another's grief to shed light on our own."

※ HUNTER BELL'S DIARY, DECEMBER 28, 1857 ※

$\mathcal{D}$espite their persecution in America, most of the Chinese never returned to their homeland. At least with breath. The migrant ships that brought the Chinese to the new land made healthy profits returning the same posthumously; it was essential to the Chinese that their bones be returned to the land of their ancestors lest their spirits wander forever in the darkness of a foreign land. Syau Lou's bones would not be sent back to China. They had decided that he was an American.

The burial was held two days after the child's death, and though it was still difficult for Quaye to walk, she insisted on attending the funeral. Hunter was pleased that she accompanied him. He was aware that his desire for her presence was more than the growing want for her company; it was a need for something far deeper. Like the soul rejoicing in the sun after a storm. Whether she had the power to heal his heart, or if, in her drawing from him the concealed truth of his pain, he had begun the healing himself he did not know. He did not care. The words of the blind man in the gospel of John came to him: *One thing I know, that, whereas I was blind, now I see.*

He felt a bond to her he had not felt with anyone since his flight west. He thought that he noticed something different in her as well, though he feared that he only imagined it. Several times he had glanced up to see her gazing at him. She would smile then shyly turn away her beautiful eyes.

The sky was overcast the day of the funeral—shrouded by a steel-gray haze that held the temperatures to below freezing. It had taken four men with pickaxes nearly the whole of the previous day to chop a cavity in the frozen earth big enough for the casket. Hunter held Quaye's arm as he helped her down to the camp. As they neared, they could hear the sounds of the funeral ritual—the ethereal scales of the Chinese flute contrasted by the heavy pounding of a drum.

The Chang family was gathered around a casket carved from the trunk of a tree, the adults dressed in sackcloth and hemp. Encircling the casket were paper objects in the shape of the things the child would desire in the next world: servants, money, houses, and horses. They would be burned atop the grave, the smoke carrying them heavenward to unite with the boy's spirit. There was also food: dried fruit and wines and a chicken, and a whole fish cooked with its head intact. The food was garnished with flowers cut from paper and impaled with sticks of incense to carry the essence of the food heavenward.

The music crescendoed then abruptly stopped. The father stoically came forward, hammer in hand, and nailed the casket tight. Then the paper offerings were lit by the elder, Lung Yan. The sky was specked with ashes as the paper burned and lifted, carried by the winter wind. When the last of the tokens were gone, the boy's father glanced at Hunter and spoke. Sonny sidled up to Hunter. "Mister Bell. Syau Lou's father asks you speak."

Hunter knew that the request was offered to him as a token of respect, for, outside of Sonny, not one of them spoke English.

He removed his hat as he stepped forward. It was the first time Hunter had stood over a grave since Rachel's. He had said nothing then. He was not sure what he would say now.

He took a deep breath. "It is the most poignant of times that we gather ourselves to grieve the loss of a little one. I am truly sorrowful for your loss," he said to the parents and they gazed at him as if they understood.

"We stand here encompassed by winter: the barren trees with their fallen leaves, the silent riverbed. Nothing is more certain in life or nature than death. We accept it as the way of things. Perhaps we are able because we have faith in spring. Yet somehow it seems different to us when death comes early. Much as we might bemoan an early winter, we feel robbed of something due. We feel cheated. Sometimes we rage. And sometimes we blame. And, in doing so, we say to God, 'My will be done, not Thine,' and we forget about the promise of spring." He glanced at Quaye. "In the cold of our soul's winter, we bury our hearts. And then we wonder why it is dark and why we feel so alone. And we risk spending so much of our lives occupied with our loss and what we have not, that we forget the beauty of what is and what we have still. And this is sometimes the greater loss."

He looked at Quaye. "This I know. There are more ways to lose a child than death. Perhaps those who lose a childhood to death are more fortunate than those who let the chalice of childhood slip from their grasp without ever drinking of it." He turned again to the mourning parents. "I am truly sorry for your loss. Syau Lou had a good mother and father. It is enough." Hunter bowed his head and stepped back next to Quaye's side, replacing his hat.

"Thank you, Mister Bell," Sonny said.

The casket was interred, then Hunter and Quaye slowly made their way back to the cabin.

CHAPTER TWENTY-ONE

A Glass Darkly

"The truth of our selves is too often blurred by the capricious image of our self-perception. I believe it is among man's greatest quests of life, not just to see life as it really is, but to see his part in it."

HUNTER BELL'S DIARY, DECEMBER 28, 1857

That night Hunter went outside and sat on the bench on the plank porch, wrapped in a heavy blanket against the biting cold. The eastern sky before him was hung with stars above the quiet spread of desert. A few lone clouds floated across the backdrop of a harvest moon. Quaye timidly opened the door, hesitant to disrupt his solitude. He glanced up at her and she could see the melancholy in his eyes.

"What you said today at the funeral was beautiful."

Hunter smiled sadly.

"I just wanted to tell you that. Good night."

Hunter raised his hand. "Would you join me?"

Quaye took his hand and sat down next to him. Hunter brought the blanket around her shoulders. She moved closer to him until their bodies touched lightly and she wondered if he noticed. Hunter's breath froze before him as he spoke.

"When we were building the cabin, I wanted the door to face my diggings. The Chinese wouldn't hear of it. They insisted that the door face east for harmonic balance. It is fortunate that I listened. I would still be buried in the snow."

"So would I," Quaye said. She looked at him. "I suppose I have never properly thanked you for saving my life. I am sorry for that. I was not sure then that I wished it saved."

He thought about her words. "What keeps you with him?" he asked.

It took a long time for her to answer. "It is my lot."

Hunter frowned. "It's not much of an answer."

"No. But maybe it's all there is."

"Have you considered returning to Ireland?"

"It is not a possibility."

"But if it were."

"No good comes from considering things that cannot be."

"I suppose you're right. Where about Ireland are you from?"

"I came from Cork."

"You do not carry much of a brogue."

"I have worked against it. Jak mocks me for it and this country hates me for it."

"It is unfortunate," Hunter said. "I think it is a beautiful tongue."

Her gratitude showed in her eyes.

"I have heard it said of Cork that the sky does not rain, it weeps."

"It is a beautiful, tragic land," Quaye said. "I love what I remember of it. At least before the famine. Ireland was a magical place to be a child. My father always said that there were sounds in Ireland you could hear nowhere else. At night the wind would sing a lullaby through the trees." She pulled the blanket tighter around her. "At night, when the wind blows, I can hear music in the desert as well."

"What kind of music?"

"A dirge. The earth singing for the dying sun." She again looked over at him. "Have you considered going back?"

Hunter said softly, "Every day."

"Yet you stay?"

"I've gone too far to go back."

"How can you be too far when one waits?"

"I might ask you the same."

"No one waits for me in Ireland."

Hunter looked down. "Hannah is better off without me. The sisters of the church are more fit to raise her." He spoke unconvincingly. "How is it that you came to be with Jak?"

"It was during the potato famine. Jak was in Ireland as an agent, selling passages on a vessel. My family was starving. Everyone was starving.

My father had gone out looking for food when he came upon Jak. Jak offered to help us all to America, but my father did not want to leave Ireland. So he offered to sell me to him."

"Your father told you this?"

"No. Jak."

"Do you believe Jak?"

Quaye did not answer immediately. "I saw him pay my father."

"That alone does not prove Jak's words." Hunter looked at her gravely. "It is precisely the lie Jak would have you believe."

"For what purpose?"

"If Jak can convince you that your existence was worthless to the one who gave you life, he will win the battle in subjecting you to his whim. Our false beliefs can be a chain to our souls. Only if we hold on to who we truly are can we be free. The danger is in the forgetting."

Quaye looked shaken. "Those were my father's last words to me. If I would remember who I am . . ."

"I can't know what went through your father's mind as he gave you up. Maybe your father knew what kind of man Jak was, maybe he didn't, but it is likely that he knew that there was no other way to help you. So he did what he had to do to give you a chance at life."

Hunter looked out into the starry night. "We do not see things in this life as they really are—only as we believe they are. It is as written in the Bible, we see through a glass darkly—but no glass is so dark, I think, as the looking glass in which we view ourselves."

"A looking glass cannot lie," Quaye said. "It is just polished glass."

"It is not the looking glass that lies. Nowhere does man err more greatly than when he looks to see the reality of who he is."

"And who are we?"

Hunter looked into her soft eyes. "We are worthy, Quaye. Worthy of life. Worthy of love. Worthy of kindness and gentleness. We are not some mistake of God or nature."

Quaye did not want Hunter to see her cry. She bowed her head, pulling the blanket above her chin.

"Until you can see yourself worthy of love, you will forever be chained. Not by Jak, or any man, but by your own perception."

He reached over and touched her hand and she grasped his tightly.

"I want to believe you. But perhaps I am too far gone."

"You may not be as far as you fear. What do you remember of your father?"

She closed her eyes and lost herself in thought. "He used to come back from the fields and his face would light when he saw me. He called me his 'little colleen.'"

"I know the pain of a father giving up his child. Could he have made that sacrifice if he did not love you?"

"I don't know," she answered simply. Quaye still held his hand and rested her other hand on top of it. The warmth of her hands enveloping his filled him with a wondrous electricity. How beautiful she is, Hunter thought. Impossibly beautiful. He suddenly realized that he was being drawn from the protective confines of his walled heart by something powerful, something as spiritual as it was physical. A strange coldness encompassed him. He took his hand from her. His voice was suddenly impassive.

"You are getting along well on your ankle."

Quaye did not understand nor like his sudden change in demeanor.

"It is nearly healed, I think."

He nodded, as if there was a tacit understanding of the ramifications of her reply. "If the sky is clear in the morning, I will be leaving."

"Leaving?" Quaye moved away from him on the bench.

"I will be taking the wagon to Salt Lake City. The hay got wet in the blizzard and there is none in town. I expect the trip will take four days. If it does not snow."

Quaye hesitantly asked, "Do you want me to be here when you return?"

Hunter was briefly silent and did not look at her when he spoke. "Yes."

"Then I will stay until then." She rose and went inside, limping a little as she walked. Hunter pulled the blanket around himself and looked out at the stars, and though he tried, he could think of nothing but her.

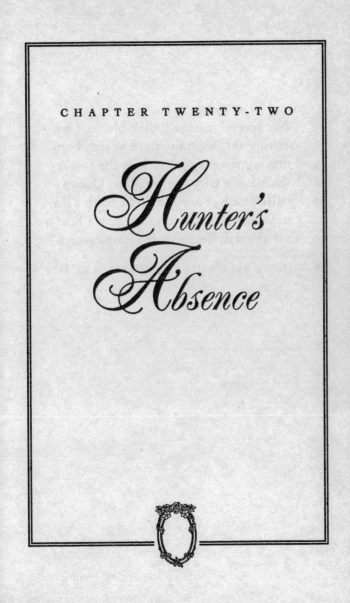

CHAPTER TWENTY-TWO

Hunter's Absence

"My scrawl is nearly illegible, as I am writing this atop the buckboard. I am driving the wagon back to the Great Salt Lake City for supplies. Quaye waits alone at my cabin. In truth I do not know what to do with her. I fear that she will be gone upon my return."

HUNTER BELL'S DIARY, DECEMBER 30, 1857

*H*unter left the next morning at dawn. Though Quaye had woken at the sound of his rising, she stayed in her bed with her eyes closed, listening to him prepare for the journey. Before he left, he came and silently stood by her. She opened her eyes to find him gazing at her.

"Be safe," she said.

He smiled at her, then he turned and left.

Emptiness filled Quaye's chest when she heard the door shut behind him. She went to the window and watched as he hitched the mules to the wagon then drove down the snow-packed trail. Her heart ached as he left her sight and she knew then the words of the poets were true, that not all pain was equal. That there could, in fact, be delicious sorrow.

Something inexplicable had happened to her the previous night. She had read in the Bible of being born again, of a mystical rebirth—and they were the only words she could think of to describe how she felt.

For the first time since she left Ireland, she began to consider that, perhaps, her life with Jak had, indeed, been based on a lie. It was as if she had wakened to a new world. But it was not her world alone; it was inseparably connected to the man who had brought her there.

Quaye went to put on her dress, but laid it aside and instead wore Hunter's flannel shirt. She boiled water and made herself a cup of tea. Sitting in the chair next to the fireplace she began to read *Wuthering Heights,* but found her mind straying and her eyes staring and not seeing. She decided instead to read from the book of sonnets, for it more closely matched the state of her emotion. Quaye went and looked out the window to be sure he had not returned, then she took Hunter's copy from the bookshelf, careful to notice how it was placed on the shelf. But even the poetry had changed for her, as it was no more in an alien tongue, but had been translated by her own heart. They had become her words. She read Rachel's inscription and wanted to sign her own name to it next to Rachel's—with all her own tender affections.

Quaye didn't believe it was possible to feel this

way about a man. She had seen couples in the New York parks walking arm in arm and that kind of mutual affection was foreign to her. She had never thought of love in the context of her own life, rather viewed it with a detached curiosity — as one views the pomp and pageantry of royal life and wonders how it might be to live it.

After an hour of reading she set aside the book and went to put the cabin in order. She began by pulling down the screen of blankets that divided her bed from the room, folding the blankets and piling them at the foot of the bed. She filled the kettle with water and gathered to the hearth whatever she deemed might benefit from a scrubbing. But even as she worked, she found her thoughts drifting to Hunter, remembering the words he used, the turn of his sentences, and as she scrubbed and arranged the evidence of his life, she suddenly wanted to know everything about his private realm, and imagined herself a part of it.

But Quaye had learned from experience that the cruelest of virtues was hope. A wall of cynicism could deflect pain, but hope opened those walls and exposed one to hurt. She never relinquished the reality that the day after Hunter's return she would be going back to Jak.

On the third day of his absence, she removed the splint. Her ankle was pale, with deep red marks impressed in her flesh where the binding had rubbed against her, but the swelling was gone. She gingerly put her full weight on it. Though it was not without discomfort, the pain was not severe. She knew it was strong enough for her return.

That afternoon a fist pounded on the cabin's door and outside a man's voice bellowed out Hunter's name. Quaye cautiously opened the door to a tall, slender man, clean shaven and boy-faced. He was dressed as finely as a dandy in a nutmeg bowler and a tan satin cravat which was carefully folded and tucked into an umber velvet waistcoat. He wore a cream-colored coat with a gold breast pin and his black Wellington boots rose nearly to his knees. The man stood a few feet from the doorway and his horse was behind him, its reins held by one of his two companions who remained perched on their mounts. One man was also dressed formally and the other was a rugged-looking man with a heavy beard, a long, tan rancher's coat, and a black felt ten-gallon hat. He wore two guns.

At the sight of Quaye the man removed his hat.

"Pardon me, ma'am. I was unaware that there was a woman on the premises."

"It is quite all right."

"I presume you are Mrs. Bell. I am looking for your husband."

Quaye did not correct him. "Mr. Bell has traveled to the Great Salt Lake City."

The man presented Quaye a calling card. "My name is Joseph Wharton. My associates and I have come all the way from California to see Mr. Bell. When do you anticipate his return?"

"I expect he'll be gone until tomorrow evening."

"Thank you, ma'am," the man said as he replaced his hat. "We shall return then. Are there particular lodgings you would recommend for the time being?"

"The only place of lodging in town is the boardinghouse. I do not know if they have vacancies."

"Would you mind if we explore the diggings?"

She uneasily glanced back at the other two men. "I suppose that would be acceptable."

He tipped his hat. "Thank you, ma'am, for your trouble."

As he walked back, his associates dismounted. The trio walked toward the creek and sluice box. Quaye shut the door and leaned against it and for reasons she did not know she felt afraid.

It was not an hour after the men left that it began to snow. The snow came sporadically at first in delicate flakes tossed by the wind's currents, then it fell thick and heavy. The temperature dropped and frost glazed the window. Quaye had plotted Hunter's journey in her mind and knew that he had likely started back to Bethel that morning. It made her anxious—a state that intensified with the snow. She began to fear that Hunter would be caught in the storm and she hoped that he had been delayed in the Great Salt Lake City, or had turned back.

The snow continued until night and then all through it, and the next morning the mountain and all its life were again silent beneath a cold shroud. And through the day Quaye prayed and worried and waited. But he did not come, that day or the next. It was Monday, only an hour before twilight, when Hunter returned.

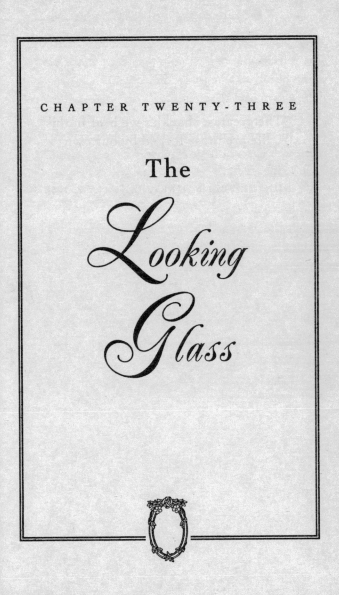

CHAPTER TWENTY-THREE

The

Looking

Glass

"The greatest shackles we bear in this life are those forged by our own fears."

✳ HUNTER BELL'S DIARY, JANUARY 7, 1858 ✳

*Q*uaye heard a mule's bray when the wagon was still fifty yards out; she watched from the window as Hunter pulled the wagon up to the snow-banked stable. Her stomach ached with the excitement of anticipation. To her disappointment he did not come right in, but set about the chores of his return. Had she known why he tarried, it would have pleased her. Hunter, too, was anxious. He had thought about Quaye constantly the last week. He had desperately wanted to get back to her and had started out Thursday morning and pushed ahead until the storm had forced him back to the city to wait out his return in a hotel until Sunday morning. Even before his first departure he had spent several hours deciding upon a suitable present for her and ended up with three. Then, delayed by the weather, he added two more. He had gotten a shave and his face felt naked. It was the face of his past. He worried that she might not like what it exposed.

On the long ride across the desert, he thought of little else but her beauty. He was not certain if the image indelibly etched in his mind was of her physical form or of the spirit it encompassed; if her eyes were lovely for their shape and hue or if it was the tenderness he saw in them. If the beauty of her lips was in their fullness, or in the way they rose as she smiled at him.

He feared she might have taken the opportunity of his absence to leave—an uncomfortable state of mind that intensified as he approached home. When he saw the smoke rising from his cabin, he felt relief and pleasure which quickly evolved into the anxiety of uncertain reunion.

He pulled the wagon into the stable and unloaded the alfalfa from the bed with a pitchfork. Then he unhitched the mules and hayed and brushed them and cleaned the frogs of their hooves. It was black outside when he went to the cabin.

He opened the door then a moment later, with his arms filled with packages, walked backward through its threshold, and closed the door behind himself. Quaye sat on the edge of the bed. They quietly stared at each other.

"I am back," he finally said, immediately realizing how foolish the declaration sounded. Quaye realized that he was clean shaven. He looked boyish, she thought, and she wanted to touch his face. Instead she smiled and motioned to her own chin. "You shaved your beard. You have a nice face."

Hunter looked embarrassed. He did not respond to her compliment.

"Those packages look heavy, come set them down."

"I brought you gifts." He lay them next to Quaye but did not sit down. "You may open them."

Quaye raised her hand to her breast. "All those are for me?"

Hunter nodded, and handed her the top present, a small tin round, its lid adorned with a hand-painting of a woman in Swiss costume, gathering meadow flowers. The canister was filled with candy: horehound and peanut brittle. Quaye smiled and lifted a piece of brittle and snapped it in half. She offered the larger of the two pieces to Hunter and placed the other in her own mouth. Though it was not often indulged, she had a fondness for sweets. Hunter gestured to the other boxes and she lay aside the open tin. She lifted the lid of another small package. Inside was a blown-glass Christmas ornament.

Hunter said, "It is past the season. I thought you would like it."

Quaye held the bauble above her head to examine it in the lantern's light.

"It is lovely." She gently set it back in its box. The next package was slightly larger and contained a hairbrush. The handle was carved from ivory and inset with three deep-purple amethysts.

"Oh, my," Quaye exclaimed. She ran her fingers across the heads of the bristles.

"This goes with it," Hunter said, handing her another box.

She lifted its lid to expose an ornate hand mirror, exquisitely cast in sterling silver.

"A looking glass." She delicately lifted it out of the box and stared into the mirror as if she had never before seen her own reflection. She finally said, "It is beautiful."

"I suppose that depends a good deal upon who gazes into it," Hunter said.

She smiled with pleasure as she lightly set the looking glass back in the box.

"I am speechless."

"There is still one more present." He handed her the largest of the boxes—a long rectangular box and the only one wrapped in paper. She tore back the white wrapping then stared at its contents in awe. Inside the box lay a dress of dark green satin.

"I hope that it fits well. I guessed at your size."

She lifted it from the box.

"There's lace to adjust the bodice." He spoke awkwardly. Soft things, feminine things, did not exist in his world of buckskin and canvas, in thought or otherwise. Nor did they in Quaye's. Hers was a life of necessity, cold and hard and sharp. For a moment she just stared at the dress as if she dare not touch it. She glanced up at him. "Where would I wear such a garment?"

"I brought back some wine and beefsteak for dinner. Perhaps you would wear it tonight. For me."

The request pleased her. "I would like to bathe before I put it on."

Bathing was not a regular ritual of the western life. It was, in fact, considered by many as unnatural or wicked. The washtub leaned in the corner of the room filled with burlap sacks of coffee and oats.

"I'll fetch the tub for you," Hunter said. "You can bathe while I prepare dinner."

Hunter removed his things from the tub and carried it to the rain barrel which had been brought inside for winter. He filled the tub partway with the soft water, then he filled two kettles and hung them both over the fire. Water sloshed over the tub's sides and onto himself as he dragged it over to Quaye's bed. While they waited for the water to heat, they rehung the blankets, sequestering the tub from the rest of the room.

"Have you soap?"

"In the pantry." Hunter retrieved a chunk of lye soap and two rags, then he went to the hearth and carried back a steaming cauldron of water and poured it into the tub. He brought over the second pot, tested the water with his wrist, and poured only half of it.

"It is a bit hot."

"I am sure that it will be fine," she said. She tugged on the curtain then excused Hunter with a smile.

He carried the kettle back to the fire then lit a candle at the table and sat down at it to prepare supper. With a buck knife he cubed a loaf of bread, mixed egg, cream, and sugar into a bowl, and poured it over the bread in the pan, setting it into the firebox to bake. He went outside and brought in carrots and squash he had kept frozen in the snow and dropped them into the half-full kettle to boil. Then he placed two large beefsteaks on a grill over the fire. He poured red wine over the meat; it ignited as it fell into the flames.

Behind the curtain, Quaye unbuttoned the flannel shirt and draped it across the bed then sat down next to it. She again lifted the silver looking glass from its wooden box. The lantern's flickering light danced off her pale skin as she gazed at the reflection of herself. With her free hand she pulled her hair up, away from her face. She let it go and it tumbled about her shoulders. Then she softly touched her own skin, drew a slender finger across her cheek, tracing her jaw. She stared at herself as if she were encountering a stranger. Quaye did not look at herself often. She did not intentionally look at herself at all. She knew that men found her attractive. They had said so in incidents she did not care to call to mind—incidents buried beneath scar tissue of bitter remembrance. As long as she could remember, her beauty had betrayed her and she did not wish to be lovely at all. Until now. For the first time that she could recall she desired to be beautiful in the eyes of a man.

She tested the bath's water with her toe then slowly stepped in. The water level rose to the brim of the tub as she closed her eyes and sank into the hot water. She did not look at herself. She wished the water could wash away every vile thought she held of her own body—a baptism to cleanse all that she had suffered. All that she was. She suddenly felt afraid. To know that only blankets separated her from *him* made her feel vulnerable. She did not want Hunter to see her. Even clothed in the beautiful dress he had brought her, she was naked and she did not want him to look on her. To pass judgment. She could not bear his rejection and surely he would reject her. If he knew what she had done, he would reject her.

She wanted to be with Jak. There was safety in Jak—a horrible, loathsome safety. Hunter had tempted her to live when death was so much safer. Then the words of a sonnet came to her: "I yield the grave for thy sake, and exchange,/ My near sweet view of Heaven, for earth and thee."

There was a gentleness to this beautiful man, she thought. And perhaps that alone made the risk worthwhile. In Hunter's service to her, he had required nothing of her. Not even her gratitude. It seemed impossible to her that this man seemed to take such pleasure in her pleasure, such joy in her joy.

Could it be that this man loved her? Though she dared not believe it, he had shown nothing to the contrary. He spoke gently to her. He had handled her heart as no man ever had—as if it were a prize of great worth, first to be won, then to be held gently as something precious. As delicate and as translucent as the ornament he had given her.

She looked down at the ring on her finger and she remembered her mother's words: May ye find love to turn it right someday. For the first time since it had been placed on her finger, she removed the silver ring, moving it from one hand to the other.

She came out of the tub, toweled herself off, then lowered the chemise over her head. She stepped into her new dress, pulled it up to her waist, and pulled its straps over her shoulders. She liked the way the satin slid across her body, how it felt against her smooth skin. She had never worn such an elegant dress—a lady's dress. She drew the lace at the bodice and it was tight at her waist, accenting the graceful lines of her figure. The fashion was for more substantial curves and Quaye felt too thin, but perhaps Hunter did not mind such things.

Quaye sat down on the bed, took her new brush, and ran it back through her hair, stroking the long strands until they fell smooth and supple. Then she lifted the looking glass, anxiously examining her face. She looked pale, she thought, and she pinched her cheeks to bring color into them.

When she had gained her nerve, she rose, standing concealed behind the blankets, as if awaiting the draw of a theater's curtain.

"I am ready," she said.

Hunter was squatting next to the fire prodding the bloody steaks with a fork. He had turned at her voice and slowly rose as she parted the veil of blankets and timidly walked out, her eyes searching his for acceptance.

Hunter could not take his eyes from her. She looked resplendent in the gown; the green satin rippled as she walked and intensified the green in her eyes. Hunter stared at her, struck with the kind of awe born of sunsets and God's greater creations.

"You are lovely."

She smiled at him gratefully, and though she dare not believe him, she wanted to. "Thank you for such a beautiful dress. It would make anyone lovely."

"The frame does not make the painting beautiful," Hunter said. He suddenly felt self-conscious. He gestured to the table.

"Please, sit down. Dinner is about ready." He went back to tend the meat.

"Your cabin has been a place of firsts. Since I came to America, no one has ever cooked a nice meal for me."

"Well, it is not difficult. You just sit and watch."

Quaye smiled as she sat down to the table.

"You cleaned my cabin."

"I hope you don't mind."

Hunter shook his head. "It needed a woman's hand."

"I should help you."

"You may read to me," he said.

The request surprised her. "What would you like me to read?"

"Whatever pleases you," Hunter said.

Quaye went to her bed and took her book of sonnets, then returned to the bench.

"I will read my favorite passage from Mrs. Browning," Quaye said as she opened the book. She recited the poem carefully, hoping to speak the words as well as they were written. She did not worry that the words might expose too much of her heart.

"If thou must love me, let it be for naught
Except for love's sake only. Do not say
'I love her for her smile . . . her look . . . her way
Of speaking gently, . . . for a trick of thought
That falls in well with mine, and certes brought
A sense of pleasant ease on such a day'—
For these things in themselves, Belovèd, may
Be changed, or change for thee,—and love, so wrought,
May be unwrought so. . . ."

She stopped as there was such silence she wondered if he was even listening.

"Or for the lay of a new dress?" Hunter asked. Quaye blushed and Hunter then continued the sonnet, reciting from memory.

". . . Neither love me for
Thine own dear pity's wiping my cheeks dry,—
A creature might forget to weep, who bore
Thy comfort long, and lose thy love thereby!

But love me for love's sake, that evermore
Thou may'st love on . . ."

He brought the bottle of wine to the table, then forked the steaks onto the pewter plates.

"I apologize for my dinnerware."

"I suspect you were not anticipating company this year," she said lightly.

He filled the glasses halfway with the wine and sat across from her, gesturing for her to start. She cut off a small piece of the steak and chewed it thoughtfully.

"You are a good cook for a man."

Hunter laughed. "Is that a compliment?"

She nodded. "I forgot to tell you that some men came to see you while you were away."

Hunter's brow creased. "What men?"

"They left their card. I set it on the mantelpiece." She stood and retrieved the card and handed it to him. "They are staying in town at the boarding-house."

Hunter examined the card and the apprehension left his face. "Perhaps they wish to buy my claim."

"Would you sell it?"

Hunter sipped his wine as he pondered it. "No. When did they come?"

"Friday. I told them you would be back on Saturday." She frowned as she thought about his extended absence. "I was so afraid that something had befallen you." She looked down. "I have thought of your words ever since you left."

"What have you thought?"

"You make me feel worthy." She did not have to explain. "It is another first, I suspect."

Hunter reached over and took her hand. As he glanced down at it he saw the wedding band. More a shackle than a band, he thought.

"Tell me about your ring. I have not seen one like it."

"It is a Claddaugh ring. The Irish have shared this ring for hundreds of years. My mother gave it to me the day I left Ireland. It is all that I have left of her. Jak wanted to pawn it in New York. It is the only thing I have ever successfully stood against Jak on."

"He backed down?"

Quaye said softly, "I told him that I would slit my own throat if he took it from me."

Her reply left Hunter momentarily speechless. Finally he asked, "Would you have?"

When Quaye did not answer, Hunter looked back down to the ring. The band was narrow and small. Carefully forged of silver was a diminutive heart with a crown above it and two hands encompassing it.

"Is there meaning to these symbols?"

"The heart represents love; the hands, faith in friendship; and the crown, loyalty. There are some who maintain that it represents the Godhead. The crown for the Father, the right hand for the Son, and the left for the Holy Ghost, all holding the human heart."

"What does 'Claddaugh' mean?"

"It is the city from which the ring originated. But it is also called an Irish wedding band as it has meaning with betrothal. It is passed on from a mother to her daughter. If it is worn on the left hand with the hands facing out it means one is still searching. If the hands face in, the wearer's heart is forever promised. The day my mother bequeathed it to me, I thought it a token of myself being given up for marriage. It was not until later, on the voyage, that I realized that she had turned it out as she placed it on my hand. I understand now what she meant, that I would find love somewhere else." She looked up at Hunter. "What of the ring you wear?"

"I wear no ring," Hunter said, lifting his hands in evidence.

"The ring you wear around your neck."

Her knowledge of it surprised him. "How do you know of it?"

"The night you brought me in . . . when you held me to keep me warm."

"You remember that night?"

"I remember some." She felt suddenly shy. "I felt the ring between us. I saw it later. Once when your shirt was off."

"It was Rachel's."

She was sorry to raise the memory. She again looked into Hunter's eyes, but it was not all pain that she saw. There was something more to his gaze, and she sensed that it had something to do with her.

"What was she like?"

"She was good. She made me believe in the divine. There were times that I would lie in bed next to her and wonder at what God had wrought in making woman. I have not felt such awe about any until . . ." Hunter stopped himself, glanced down to where her hand rested on his—where the ring resided. "You did not say what it means if the ring is worn on the right hand."

Suddenly she felt as wanting as she felt vulnerable. Looking into his eyes she felt safe in his gaze. "If it is worn on the right hand it means that there are possibilities for love."

Hunter gently cradled her chin in his hand and moved her face toward his own as he leaned forward and their mouths met, gently at first, then Hunter pressed her to him and Quaye moved into him. She had spent her life resisting, struggling to withhold whatever she could, and now she wanted to surrender herself to this man and the emotion she felt at this moment.

Suddenly Quaye broke away from him. She looked into his bewildered face with wild eyes, then stood and ran outside. Hunter followed her out and found her on the porch. She held her face in her hands as she sobbed.

"What's wrong, Quaye?" He touched her and she recoiled. "Is it because you are married? A covenant against one's will is of no effect."

She did not answer.

"Tell me what I have done wrong. I know I am awkward. I have not been with a woman for such a long time. I would not hurt you."

She did not look up. Her voice fell anguished. "Leave me, Hunter. Please leave me."

His chest constricted. "I will leave if you wish. But you must let me know why."

"I am not your good Rachel. You do not know me. You do not know my darkness."

"There is no darkness in you."

"You do not see it, because you do not know me."

"I can discern your spirit. And what I see is pure and innocent."

"Then you do not see as clearly as you believe."

He moved closer to her to take her in his arms again, but she moved away from him.

"In you I see a woman who is more holy and nearer to God than I with my seminary and covenants ever came to be. There is more divinity in you in rags than the pious ones in the holy vestments of the church."

"You don't know. You don't know the darkness inside of me." She looked up, her face wet with tears and contorted in pain. "We do what is expected of us, Hunter. As loathsome and vile as it may be, we do fall to it."

Her words were a white cloud in the winter air. After a moment Hunter asked, "What do you fear me to know?"

She looked steadfastly into his eyes. "If I tell you, where will I reside in your heart?"

"I don't know, Quaye. But you must have faith in me."

Her head fell as if the truth had become too weighty to withhold any longer. When she looked up there was great sadness in her eyes.

"Jak was so cruel when we arrived in America. There was so much hatred for the Irish immigrants in New York. For us Catholics. The hatred fueled Jak. He knew, we both knew, that this new world would crush me." She wiped at her eyes. "Jak beat me at the slightest provocation, sometimes without any. It didn't matter where. If we were in our flat or on the street, or in the market, he would beat me just to remind me that he could. If I didn't do everything the way he wanted, his temper would flare and I would wait as he would devise my punishment. Sometimes that would be the greater punishment, the not knowing. I would beg his forgiveness. He liked me to beg. I would despise myself for it but still I did it." She was trembling. Hunter wanted to hold her to comfort her but she would not allow him near her.

"Jak could not find work. He would not sail again. He would not leave me. He said that there was no work in the dockyards because all the Irish immigrants would work for just a pint of beer and had taken the work from the real Americans. I didn't know if it was true. I didn't know if anything he said was true, but it didn't matter. I was just so weak and so afraid. I don't know how he did it, but somehow he took my mind. And he owned it and he tortured it and we both knew that there was nothing I could do about it.

"I began to believe that it was my fault that he was so often angry with me. When I apologized, when I begged his forgiveness, I believed that I deserved whatever he did to me because I had failed to please him. I believed that he was always right and that I could do nothing without him. I feared not only him, but life without him telling me what to do. In New York he sent me to work as a millgirl while he would spend the money I made in the pubs. After work, I would make his dinner, then I would wait until he came home and tell me that I could eat. One time he was in a dark mood and he poured the stew I made off his plate and he told me to eat it off the floor. I asked him why. I said, 'Why are you making me eat off the floor?' and he grabbed my hair and pulled me to my knees in front of it, then he pushed my face in it and said because he had said to. And because dogs eat off the floor and I was an Irish dog. I tried to understand but I couldn't. He made me nothing, then he hated me for being nothing."

Quaye was sobbing and for a moment could neither speak nor look at Hunter. When she looked again into his eyes there was an unusual distance to her gaze. "One night Jak brought home a strange man. I don't know where he came from. . . ." At this she paused and turned from Hunter and her voice quivered. "Jak told me to disrobe in front of the man. But I couldn't. He threatened to beat me to death and I told him to go ahead and be done with it. He was going to kill me someday anyway. The man told Jak to leave me be and to give him his money back. That just made Jak more angry. He came at me and he tore off my clothing. I just stood there. I let him do it. I didn't care anymore. It was as if I had left my body, as if I had died and there was nothing to look on but a corpse. The man had paid Jak money to look on me and Jak let him. Somehow that pleased both of them." Her words came slowly now. "But it was only the beginning. He brought other men. He would meet them in the saloons. There were many men. I don't know how many. I have tried to forget . . . but they . . ." She looked back at Hunter and the darkness of her eyes frightened him. "You see? I am sinful and vile. Would you take me now, knowing this?"

All was silent except for Quaye's muffled sobs. Hunter took her hand and this time she did not resist.

"The sin in this is on Jak's head, not yours."

"But would you take me?"

If anything, what she had been forced to do only made Hunter want her more, to care for her. It aroused every manful instinct to protect her, to hold her, and to love her. But to take her? It was only then that he realized the weight of the chains that held him bound to the past; the sure, terrible shackles of fear, made more powerful by his feelings for her.

Hunter did not answer—he could not answer her, and as he silently gazed at her, he saw the light in her eyes, the dim, flickering candle of her renewed spirit, flicker and die. And it was as if he was with Rachel again, in the darkened room, kneeling at her bedside; the life draining from her eyes, her voice faint and tremorous. The terror of his failure at her side held him helpless and still. Quaye did not cry anymore, but turned away from him and silently went back inside. For the first time in his life Hunter truly felt damned.

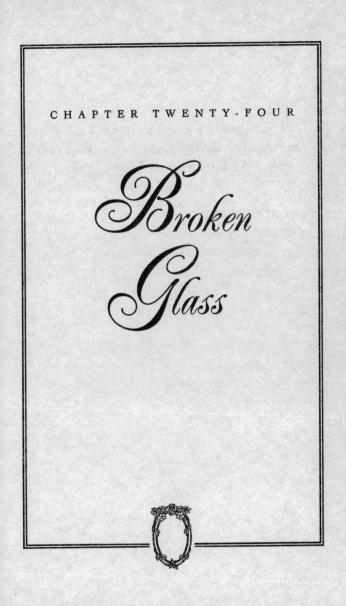

CHAPTER TWENTY-FOUR

Broken Glass

"I have made a grave mistake. I have carelessly handled a heart entrusted to mine. And in so doing I have broken both."

❊ HUNTER BELL'S DIARY, JANUARY 7, 1858 ❊

*H*unter woke early the next morning; in truth he had barely slept. He quietly left the cabin before dawn to hunt. In part to think, in part to avoid the blistering silence of Quaye's hurt. He knew he had failed her at the most crucial of moments. As he trudged through the snow, he considered what he would say when he went back, wondering if there was anything that could be said with any effect. The more he thought on it the more he hated himself for what he had done.

He shot a wild turkey, carried the bird back to his barn, and began to pluck it, welcoming the monotony of the operation as a relief from his tortured thoughts. He was no closer to knowing what he would say.

The whinny of an approaching horse brought him to the door of the stable. Riding up the snow-packed trail was Jak Morse.

"Bell," he shouted.

Hunter lifted his gun and walked toward the rider. He recognized Jak and fingered the trigger on the gun. He had never before wanted to kill a man, but now he considered dropping Morse right there.

"Word in town is that ya got a woman up here."

"What I have is none of your concern."

"An Irishwoman."

Hunter pulled back the bolt on his rifle as he stepped toward him. "There's nothing here that belongs to you. Now get off my property unless you wish to be buried here."

Neither Jak nor Hunter himself questioned the reality of the threat. Morse was about to retreat when the door to the cabin opened and Quaye stepped out into the sunlight. She did not look at Hunter as she calmly walked out onto the porch, her arms wrapped around herself for warmth. She wore only the dress that she had been found in, now neatly mended. Except for the boots, she had nothing that Hunter had given her. Both men stared at her.

"I've come to get you," Jak shouted.

Quaye did not reply, but, with her head slightly bowed, started toward the horse. Hunter could not believe what he was seeing. He stepped in her path and grasped her arm but she pulled it free without looking at him. "Where are you going?"

Her reply was calm and composed. "Back to where I belong."

"You don't belong to him, Quaye. You deserve more."

"Do I now?"

"Can't you see he is evil? He is cruel."

She turned to him and her face was twisted with a strange smile, as if his last statement amused her. "Oh, Hunter. You are far crueler than Jak. At least he never led me to believe that he loved me."

She stepped aside of him and walked to the horse.

"Quaye."

She did not turn back. Without word Jak lifted her up and then looked at Hunter, an arrogant smile on his face. Quaye sat sidesaddle looking away from Hunter. Jak reared the horse then kicked it and they rode back toward town. Hunter stood stunned with disbelief; his chest throbbed. He went back inside and to her bed and angrily tore down the blankets from the partition.

Everything he had bought for her was still there. The books were stacked at the foot of the bed and the satin dress had been carefully folded next to the brush and ornament. Everything was replaced in its original container except for the looking glass, which lay at the foot of the bed. And it was shattered.

CHAPTER TWENTY-FIVE

News

"Again, I am encompassed by walls of solitude. I believe that Hell must be a confinement of our own contrivance, laid brick by brick, until, by our own cowardice and compromise, we have isolated ourselves from all love. And from all that is lovely."

❉ HUNTER BELL'S DIARY, JANUARY 8, 1858 ❉

*Q*uaye filled Hunter's mind, in and over and around it. If his feelings for her were not sufficient to tumble the walls that he had built around his heart then it was obvious that she had entered through the back gate. His memory of her was as pervasive as the pain that now filled it. He saw her in everything that surrounded him. At each whisper of wind or snap of tree, he would glance up hoping she had returned.

Over the next two days, he revisited the night, remembering the tenderness of Quaye's hand on his. He remembered her kiss and how it had filled and warmed his world, and felt the cold starkness of her absence. He had hurt her deeply and he now atoned for her pain with each tortured moment of his own loneliness. Still, it was not his own loss that brought him the greatest anguish, but the realization of what Quaye had returned to. What he had compelled her to return to.

He worked to exorcise the thoughts with physical labor. He felled two trees and dragged them back to his cabin where he chopped them into firewood, splintering log after log until even the callouses on his hands began to blister.

On the second day, as the sun neared its zenith, he heard the clop of an approaching horse and he went with his ax in hand to see who had come. He hoped that it might somehow be her.

To Hunter's disappointment, it was an old man astride a graying mule, his manner of dress clearly denoting him as a forty-niner. He wore a flimsy, wide-brimmed hat and beneath his coat a crimson, open-neck woolen shirt. His trousers were tucked into his boots.

The man stopped the mule. "Are ya Bell?"

Hunter leaned against the ax. "Yes."

"Name's Jon Billings. I just come to Bethel." The old man looked out over Hunter's claim, seemingly in no more hurry to speak than the mule had been in its approach. "I done a lifetime of pannin', two more of lode minin'. I'm lookin' fer work. I know ya ain't diggin' now, but if ya can see your way to spot me the most meager lay, come spring I'll make it up to ya."

"I've got plenty of help," Hunter replied tersely.

"They say in town that ya just got Johnnies workin'."

Hunter did not respond.

"Like I said, I come lookin' fer work."

Hunter asked, "Where did you ride from?"

"Came in from just north a ways. Goldstrike."

"I prospected in Goldstrike."

"How'd ya make out?"

"I'm here."

The man smiled, took a burnt cigar from his pocket, offered it to Hunter, who refused, then lit it and expelled a cloud of blue smoke. "Sodom West the papers call it. Got that right."

"Do you know the Orleans boardinghouse?"

"Never had occasion to bed there, but I know it. They changed the name on it. It's the Red Eye boardinghouse now. That Cajun who used to own it got real drunk and shot up one of the saloons and a couple of its occupants pretty severe. They jailed him for a spell. Made him pay for fixin' up the saloon. Had to sell his place. Cajun been loco ever since his girl's murder."

Hunter stared at him in stunned disbelief. "What happened to his girl?"

"What was her name?" He thought on it a moment then shook it off. "Anyway, big news round Goldstrike. One of her own boarders done her in. Shot her up good."

"Isabel," Hunter said.

"That's right. Mulatto girl. They say she were pretty as a fawn."

"Did they hang her murderer?"

"No. Man stole her horse and hightailed it out of Goldstrike before they caught him. They say he was a preacher man gone to the devil. Vigilantes was the ones who found her. They were already on to the man. They 'spect other foul play, ladyfolk being scarce and all in Goldstrike. The vigilance committee put up a fair reward on that preacher's head, but I 'spect he's to the Yukon by now."

Hunter turned away.

" 'Bout the work . . ."

"Like I said, I don't need any help."

"Not askin' for much lay."

"I'm not offering any."

"Ya got work for a Chinaman but not a white man?"

"I reckon so."

The man returned the cigar to his mouth and pulled back on the mule's reins. "That kind of thinkin' bound to get a man in trouble," he said. He and the mule slowly retraced the path they had come up.

✳

Hunter was still reeling from the news of Isabel's death several hours later when three men approached on horseback. When they were within speaking distance the tallest of the threesome spoke. "I presume you are Hunter Bell."

"You have the advantage."

The man climbed down from his horse, walked toward Hunter. "I spoke with your wife just before that storm hit. Spent the last three days in this god-forsaken desert." He offered his calling card. "Joseph Wharton's the name. I represent the Comstock Mining Company of San Francisco. This is Mr. Barton, our geologist, and Mr. Greeley, our guide. We have heard tale of your claim. Mr. Barton here has investigated your diggings and set store by the accounts. We would like to bring in hydraulics and follow the vein into the mountain. We are prepared to make you an offer on your claim."

"Make it."

"The Comstock Company is prepared to offer you one half of a million dollars and five percent stock in the Bethel Mining Company."

Hunter was nonplussed by the amount. Not because he had brought out a quarter of that already, but because gold seems insignificant to a broken heart.

"I had not planned on selling."

"I know about you, Mr. Bell. You are a civilized man. What would make a man like you want to stay in a place like this?"

"How would the transaction take place?"

"We could wire the money to a bank of your choosing. Or we could plank down in cash, but I don't think that would be prudent, considering the environment."

"I need time to think on it."

Wharton smiled. "Your hesitance pleases me. It shows confidence in your diggings." The man returned to his horse. "Our board of directors meets next Thursday. I would like to telegraph your reply the preceding day." He climbed back into the saddle. "We are lodged at the Bethel boardinghouse. Decision or not, we will be leaving the Monday next."

CHAPTER TWENTY-SIX

Three
of a
Kind

"Nowhere is royalty less to be trusted
than in a deck of cards."

❉ HUNTER BELL'S DIARY, JANUARY 10, 1858 ❉

It took Hunter less than an hour to pack everything he valued. In the five months since he had come to Bethel he had cached a significant amount of gold: two leather pokes weighing nearly twenty pounds apiece. Even without selling his claim he was rich, rich enough to live out his life without ever again turning a card or a shovel. He could live like a king in Mexico, on a thousand-acre hacienda with a thousand head of cattle.

He would leave to the Chinese his wagon and animals and whatever he could not carry on his horse. The money from the claim would be sent to Hannah; she would want for nothing. He would make one final stop at the Chang camp to say good-bye, then ride to the boardinghouse to close the deal.

He was greeted by Sonny as he rode his horse into the camp.

"Hello, Mister Bell. You go someplace?"

"Mexico."

Sonny looked perplexed. "Mexico?"

"I am leaving," Hunter said.

"Leaving? This is bad," he said, shaking his head in disbelief. "I tell others."

The Changs did not conceal their sadness. Syau Lou's mother went to her tent and pressed on him a necklace of jade beads. At the family's insistence, he sat with them for dinner, and as he left their camp twilight ebbed into darkness. It was too late to make much of a ride; but it did not matter. With or without the sun, he would be done with Bethel. The street was dark as he rode his horse to the boardinghouse, though its windows were ablaze with light. As he approached the building he remembered his flight from Goldstrike. He had then, too, made the boardinghouse his final destination on his way out of town. And he thought again of Isabel.

Though he found having a price on his head unsettling, the news of Isabel's murder had filled Hunter more with rage than fear for his implication in it. She had come to his rescue and been forced to pay for it with her life. As Hunter remembered the details of the day, and her request to take her with him, he felt dirty—as if her blood were on his hands.

For his own fear he had run from her. Just as he had with Hannah. Just as he had with Quaye.

In that moment the loathing he felt for the vigilantes was matched by that which he felt for himself.

He glanced down the darkened street toward the lit saloon, then back at the boardinghouse.

He could run. He knew how to run. Just as he could have left Quaye to the wolves, he could leave her to the animal with whom she now lived and hope that with enough time and liquor his memory of her would die.

Or he could choose life. At that pivotal moment, it occurred to him that with all his schooling in theology he had, perhaps, missed the entire point of his studies, the very crux of the gospel he had professed to believe. That the measure of a person's heart, the barometer of good or evil, was nothing more than the extent of their willingness to choose life over death. That the path of God was, simply, the path of life, abundant and eternal. And this is where he failed, for to choose life is to choose sorrow as well as joy, pain as well as pleasure. When Hunter had buried Rachel, he buried along with her his heart, lest it might heal and feel and grow again. And in so doing he had chosen more than death, he had chosen damnation itself, for damnation is nothing more than to stop a thing in its eternal progression. In that first flight from West Chester he had run not only from the horror and pain of death but from life itself.

Hunter fully realized his own death. He had rationalized that others were better off without him. But he was wrong. He had left debts that others would pay for, and this was something he could not live with. He coaxed his horse down the street to the saloon.

Hunter had only been in the saloon once, when he had rescued Lau Jung. The room was about 40 feet long, with a long mahogany bar. A brass foot rail ran the length of it and there was a spittoon every six feet. Behind the counter was a large mirror set in a mahogany cabinet with shelves supporting stacked bottles and decanters of Scotch whisky, wheat whiskey, rye, brandy, Old Bourbon, and other liquors, including an oaken barrel of a concoction they called tangleleg. It was so potent that it was said one would be less confused to be struck by lightning than to drink it, and better off. Across from the bar, in the center of the room, was a potbellied stove with a scuttle and coal shovel to one side and a cord of wood stacked to the other. The barkeep wore a straw hat and sat behind his bar sucking on a cigar, waiting for his next customer. There were a half dozen round tables in the room but the bar was nearly empty and only one of the tables was in use. Quaye had said Jak could be found here every night and she was right. He and three other men sat playing poker at a table littered with empty bottles. Jak turned to see what the others looked at. He scowled. "What ya want?"

"I came to play cards."

"Game's closed."

"If he got spondulicks, this chair's empty," said the man seated next to Jak. He was a squat, barrel-chested man who, from the size of the stack of coins in front of him, looked to be winning.

Hunter removed his coat as he took the chair across from Jak.

"You're the preacher, ain't ya?"

Hunter extended his hand. "Hunter Bell."

"Glad to know ya. I'm Jon." He pointed to his companions. "Nate 'n Abrahm. Ya know Jak."

Hunter acknowledged the men with a slight nod. "I haven't played for a while. Least not much outside monte. But I'm sure you boys can catch me up."

The men tacitly glanced to each other, lustful for the stack of coins Hunter had set on the table. "What are we playing?"

"Draw poker," said the man.

Hunter raised a hand to the bar. "Bring us a bottle of rye."

"Can't say nuthin' 'bout that," said Jon.

The bartender brought a bottle to the table with a glass for Hunter. Hunter poured the men's glasses then his own, then took a long drink and loudly exhaled.

"Whose deal?" Hunter asked.

Jak took the deck and began sliding the cards across the table. The game moved quickly. As the men had hoped, Hunter's pile fell, though most had moved across the table to Jak, whose dour mood had changed with his fortune. Jak could not remember the last time he had been that lucky at cards and decided that—the business with his wife aside—Hunter was not such a bad fellow after all. Hunter continued to drink and the effect of the alcohol was evident to all at the table. Twice Hunter double anted.

"Preacher don't hold his liquor well," said Jon.

"I probably have had too much," Hunter agreed as he poured himself another glass. The game went on late as all the men stayed in for the fleecing, patiently waiting for their share of the kill. Around two in the morning Jak said jauntily, "Well I'm right glad ya come."

Hunter had pushed away his glass and now nursed the bottle. "I haven't done too well for myself tonight," he said dolefully.

Jak said, "Ya have 'bout as much to learn 'bout cards as ya do womenfolk."

Hunter removed the bottle from his lips. "Enlighten me."

"Well, ya got it all wrong. A woman's same as a nigger. Respects a strong hand. If ya don't break 'em they'll give ya nothin' but trouble. Ya can't go filling her head with books and religion and the like. It's against her nature. Womenfolk just born to think about young'uns and takin' care of their menfolk." He bit down on the end of his cigar and smiled at Hunter. "Any man let a woman have her way ain't a man. He's a gelding."

The men snickered.

Hunter rubbed his forehead. "I'm not much at cards, but I'm at odds with you about women."

"Which is why my woman came a scurryin' back as soon as I came for her. They just askin' for a man to put 'em right. A woman's proper place is on her back. She'll only respect the man who can put her there."

Hunter hid his contempt as he leaned back in his chair and examined his remaining stack of coins. "I think I have enough for one more hand. Let's see if I can win any of it back. I believe it's my deal."

Jak happily pushed the deck to him and the men anted up. Hunter took another drink from the bottle then dealt. As the cards slid across the table, Jak stared stone-faced at his hand. He had collected three kings—his best hand of the night. They commenced to check and raise until, by the third round, the other three men had folded. Jak continued to raise until Hunter pushed the last of his gold into the pot.

"Guess that's it," Hunter said despondently. "Money's on the table."

"Ya look confident in that hand," Jak said.

Hunter nodded warily. "Might be."

"I'd be willin' to take a note."

Hunter tapped his cards on the table. "You'll take a note." Hunter considered the prospect then asked, "Have you a pen?"

Jak shouted to the bartender, "Git a pen."

The bartender brought a piece of paper and a metal pen. Hunter scrawled a note then took another drink, shaking his head from its potency. He pushed the paper toward Jak.

"Cain't read but numbers. I ain't see any on this here paper."

"It's a deed for my claim."

Jak stared at it incredulously. "Now I might be a touch richer tonight on 'count of your generosity, but I heard 'bout that claim of yours. What am I gonna raise against that piece a paper?"

"Your wife."

Jak gazed at him in amused disbelief, then glanced to the others at the table. He laughed nervously. "Ya want my wife?"

"My claim against your wife."

"Ya get tired of them Chinawomen?" he asked mockingly.

"If you're not interested . . ." Hunter reached for the deed but Jak quickly laid his hand on the paper. "Didn't say I ain't willin' to play it. Ya men all a witness to this."

Jon protested. "He's drunk, Jak."

"Not so drunk he cain't play," Jak said.

"I got my faculties," Hunter said, his words slightly slurred.

"There, ya heard it," Jak said.

Hunter turned the paper and pushed it toward him. "Now write it down."

"Cain't read, sure as hell cain't spell."

"I'll do it for you." Hunter wrote down the terms of the wager, showed it to Jon, who nodded, then pushed it back toward Jak. "Now sign it."

Jak crossed an X then leaned back in his chair. "Then it's done. I call ya."

"You turn first," Hunter said.

A broad smile stretched Jak's face. "I tell ya. Ya been playin' like an ass. A right gen'rous ass, but an ass all the same. It only right ta let ya onta a secret."

"What's that?"

"Seems ya got a habit. When ya bluffin' ya stack them coins right on top a your cards." He turned over his three kings. "That makes me a rich man."

"No," Hunter said, "that makes you a lone one."
To the men's astonishment Hunter's diction was
suddenly sharp and his eyes clear and stone-cold
sober. He turned over three aces. "Even asses get
lucky now and then."

"Well I'll be cussed," said one of the men. Jak's
smile disappeared. He stared in disbelief as Hunter
pulled in his deed and coins and stood. "I want her
at my place before noon." He leaned over the table
and his eyes were fierce. "If you value your pathetic
life, there won't be any fresh marks on her." Then
he turned and left the saloon.

CHAPTER TWENTY-SEVEN

Quaye's Choice

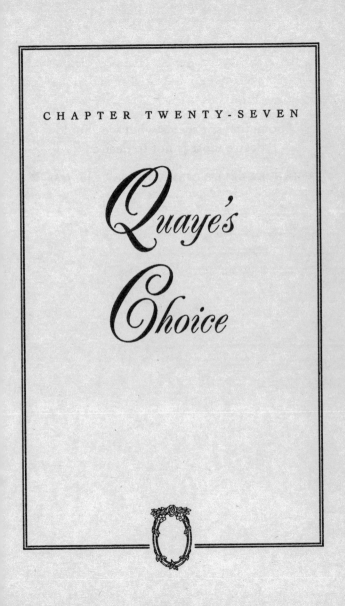

"Sometimes it seems what we should desire most is not to desire."

❊ HUNTER BELL'S DIARY, JANUARY 10, 1858 ❊

he sun was high in a cloudless sky and the snow melted and trickled down the mountainside in small runoffs. Quaye carefully stepped over and between the rivulets as she climbed the foothills to Hunter's cabin. It was an hour before noon when she pushed open the cabin's door. She had walked from town carrying the whole of her life's possessions in a small oilcloth tied with a sash which draped across her back and diagonally across her chest. Hunter had anxiously awaited her arrival, had played through his mind what he might say, what he ought to say, and the only thing he had settled on was an apology. He was whittling the bedpost as she arrived. When he heard her outside he set aside his knife, leaving the wood in small, curled shavings at the foot of the bed.

Quaye stepped inside, untied the pack, and laid it a few feet from the doorway. She stared at him from across the room. The sun at her back made a halo around her.

"What right have you to play with my life?" she asked angrily.

Hunter did not reply.

"Did you think you could buy me?"

"I did not buy you."

"No, you won me in a card game. At least Jak paid cash."

"I did not buy you. Only your freedom." He slowly rose from the floor, his eyes locked on hers. "I am sorry for what I did. More so for what I didn't do. The night I found you in the snow, I believed that God had sent you to torment me. To relive the pain I felt in losing Rachel." He looked down, flustered with the awkwardness of his words. "I know I hurt you. If I had to do it over I would not make the same mistake."

Quaye silently gazed at him. She finally said, "I cannot be her."

"It is you who I love."

"You love me? Until when? Until the pain of remembrance returns and you run to a new town? What would be left of me then?"

"I will not leave you."

"You already have, Hunter."

"Please give me another chance."

Quaye looked down. "I can't."

"Then release me. Tell me that you don't love me."

Quaye began to cry. "That is why I cannot give you another chance. I have never loved nor feared anyone as I do you. I wish that you had let me die that night."

Hunter took a deep breath and, with the words still stinging in his heart, walked to the corner of the cabin. He crouched down amidst a stack of wooden boxes then returned holding a small leather purse. He held it out to her. "There is enough for your return east. Or to Ireland."

Quaye would not touch it. She wiped her eyes. "I cannot be in your debt."

His voice softened until it came naked and pleading. "Quaye, I deserve whatever hell you choose for me. I don't know if I can take you leaving me again, but that isn't my choice anymore. I know that I would rather die a thousand deaths than to see you with Jak again. I ask . . . no, I beg just this one thing. Take this money and go as far from here as you can. If you ever felt anything for me, give me just this to ease the pain I will feel for the rest of my life. Let me know that you are not with him."

Quaye looked into Hunter's eyes. She took the purse and turned from him. Pausing indecisively for a moment, she bent over and retrieved her own duffel then walked out of the cabin. When the door shut, Hunter went to his pantry, took out a brown jug of brandy, and began to drink.

CHAPTER TWENTY-EIGHT

The

Lynching

"It is a peculiar justice they practice in the West; a mockery of the law overseen by the dishonorable judge Lynch with his 10,000 arms and two bum eyes."

HUNTER BELL'S DIARY, SACRAMENTO, 1856

*H*unter was fully dressed under his blankets staring at the dark timbers of his roof's underbelly when Sonny came. He had lain in bed for nearly three days, drinking the whole of the jug and two other bottles. The room reeked of alcohol and vomit.

Sonny had come to feed the livestock when he noticed Hunter's horse in the corral. He called out, then, when he got no response, he slowly opened the cabin door. At first he thought the room vacant, as there was neither motion nor light. The fire had gone out, leaving the cabin in a bitter chill that clouded his breath. Then he saw Hunter's form in bed and he went to his side. Hunter had a hand on his forehead as he lethargically turned toward him.

"Mister Bell, are you sick?"

Hunter did not immediately respond. "No. Maybe."

Sonny spied the bottles. "You drink too much whiskey."

"Not enough."

Sonny went to the hearth and began to rekindle the fire. "Why you not go to Mexico?"

"I did not sell the mine. You can still keep what I gave you."

"We happy you not go," Sonny said. "I tell family. We have feast for you."

"No feast," Hunter said.

Sonny struck a match and the fire caught. "I bring Lung Yan. He know Chinese medicine."

"I don't suppose he has something for melancholy."

"Melancholy," Sonny echoed. Suddenly his eyes widened. "Irishwoman?"

"Yes," Hunter said and it was almost a sigh. "The Irishwoman."

"I make you tea for bad head." Sonny foraged through Hunter's provisions while he waited for the water to boil. He was startled by the report of a rifle.

"Hunter Bell!" a man hollered. Hunter did not move. He lay still as if he had not heard the call. Sonny went to the window and drew back its curtain. "Two men come," Sonny reported. "The bad man come."

"Get my gun," Hunter said. "It's by the shelf."

He climbed out of bed and his head spun. He stood still until the cabin stopped its pirouette. He slowly opened the door and a beam of light pierced the room. He shielded his eyes from the sun. When his eyes adjusted to the light he saw Jak accompanied by a large, grim-faced man wearing a black-banded straw hat and holding a shotgun at his waist. Hunter knew him by reputation and badge as Sheriff Ponds.

Hunter pulled on his boots then stepped outside. Jak was pointing out the Appaloosa in the corral.

"What do you want?" Hunter asked. The men turned to him.

"There's the murderin' horse thief," Jak said.

The sheriff leveled his shotgun in Hunter's direction. "Bell, I am arresting you for the killing of Isabel Gayarre."

Hunter held his head. "Isabel was my friend. The Goldstrike vigilantes killed her."

"The vigilantes found her."

"Of course they did. After they murdered her."

"The day Isabel Gayarre was found dead, you disappeared from Goldstrike with her horse. This here Appaloosa fits the description."

"It is Isabel's horse. I bought it from her."

"With a slug," Jak interjected.

"Isabel was helping me escape from the vigilantes and they killed her for it."

"This will be tried in court," Ponds said. "Now come along."

❈

It did not take more than two days for word of the preacher's arrest to reach Goldstrike. Ponds had sent to the Goldstrike sheriff for identification of Isabel's horse, and word that a trial was imminent spread through the town. While most of Goldstrike celebrated the news of Hunter's capture, Isabel's murderer, Thomas Cage, feared it.

Cage, accompanied by another vigilante, had shot Isabel when he learned that she had abetted Hunter's escape. It was with good reason that he was afraid. Isabel was beloved in the town and Cage knew that if either her father, the townspeople, or even some of his own vigilantes were convinced of someone's guilt in her death, be it the Almighty Himself, they would take gun or rope to settle the matter. The town had accepted Cage's story of the preacher's crime, and he had counted on never seeing Hunter again. The large bounty on the preacher's head, to which he had contributed, should have ensured that. Cage suspected that Hunter and Isabel had been lovers and he feared Hunter might hold evidence that could prove his innocence and subsequently indict Cage.

It was Cage's intent that Hunter's evidence never be presented. A bulletin was hastily posted in the town's saloons and banks.

VIGILANCE COMMITTEE

The members of the Goldstrike Vigilance Committee in good standing will please meet at the Virginian Saloon tomorrow at noon with regards to the capture of the notorious Hunter Bell, murderer of Isabel Gayarre

---

The vigilantes, in good standing or otherwise, were excited by news of Hunter's capture and turned out in droves. Cage fanned their indignation until it was combustible, inciting them with talk that Bethel was the kind of town that would let the preacher walk after murdering one of Goldstrike's best. "Mark my words," Cage warned. "With a demon's tongue he'll talk his way outta it."

By the end of the hour the crowd unanimously agreed that the only decent thing for law-loving citizens to do was to take this matter into their own hands.

✳

It was an hour before dusk on Hunter's fourth day of incarceration when the deputy rushed into the Bethel jailhouse. He barred the door behind him, and an anxious discussion ensued between him and the sheriff. Hunter leaned forward against the long bars of his cell, trying to determine the source of the men's agitation. Outside his window, the clamor of horses and men shouting rose as a gathering took place. From the sound of the din, Hunter guessed the crowd at forty to fifty men.

The sheriff brought down two shotguns from the gun rack on the wall and loaded them both, keeping a box of ammunition nearby. Neither lawman spoke to the prisoners but they were clearly fearful. Hunter sensed it had something to do with him.

The commotion climaxed with a succession of gunshots and the crowd suddenly fell silent, followed by the sound of one man's voice directed at the jail.

"Open the door, Sheriff."

Hunter thought he recognized the voice. The sheriff shouted back, "You boys just go on back to Goldstrike. We have law in Bethel."

"This ain't your man, Sheriff. The preacher belongs to the Goldstrike vigilance committee. We ain't no puke murderer sympathizers. We ain't leavin' here without a hangin'."

A higher-pitched voice hollered, "We just

brought a new collar for the preacher. A hempen one."

Hunter held the bars of his cell.

"Can't do it, boys. Now just settle on down before somebody gets hurt."

"We reckon that's just what we came for," said the latter voice. The statement was cheered by the crowd.

The sheriff's voice was heavy with stress, "Listen, boys, your blood is up. If you're up to a hangin' then I'll just send out Barberi. He's goin' to be hung in the morning anyhow."

Barberi was an ill-tempered Italian miner who had been jailed for shooting a man because he didn't like the way he looked at him. He was slumped down against the back wall of the cell across from Hunter, nursing a bottle of whiskey. He showed no emotion at the sheriff's offer.

"We come for the preacher," shouted the man. "Now you just come outta there so you don't get hurt. We'll burn the place down if we have to."

A rifle ball pierced the door and embedded itself in the wall behind, raining small fragments of plaster to the stone floor.

The deputy's voice rose. "That preacher's just gonna be hung in the end anyhows. May as well let the vigilantes do it and save a lot of paper. Wash your hands of it, Sheriff."

The sheriff sat quietly for a moment then glanced back at Hunter. "I am powerful sorry," he said. "God have mercy on your soul."

"And yours," Hunter replied.

The sheriff slowly turned back, then shouted out the window, "Casey and I are comin' out. Hold your fire."

"Don't shoot," ordered the voice. "Don't forget them keys, Sheriff."

The lawmen cautiously opened the door then walked out, leaving the jailhouse open. It was only an instant before a horde of men poured in like a swarm of angry yellow jackets. At first the throng pressed toward Barberi until one of the vigilantes who knew Hunter set them straight. The sight of the bloodthirsty men filled Hunter with terror. He went to the door of his cell and vainly tried to wrest the cell key from its holder as it was inserted, then, unsuccessful at this, he wrapped his arms between the bars of the door and its threshold, but the men pounded his arms and hands with their gun butts and the door was forced open. Hunter was quickly set upon by a dozen men and dropped to his stomach on the stone floor. His hands were lashed behind his back then they pulled him to his feet and pushed him out of the cell.

Even before Hunter reached the jail's outer door, a noose had been dropped over his neck and pulled tight. The crowd led him by the rope leash. Outside the jail, Hunter recognized some of the mob. There was a score from Goldstrike's vigilance committee, but nearly as many collected from Bethel, drawn into the lynching by right of the vigilantes' fervor and their misguided indignation. The man directing the mob was, as Hunter expected, Thomas Cage. Hunter also saw Jak in the thick of it. The horde moved Hunter along, kicking him and jabbing him with their guns.

There was a brief dispute over where the hanging should take place. Some argued that Hunter should be taken back to Goldstrike and hanged, but Cage was eager to get it over with and prevailed with the promise that the preacher's head would be brought back to Goldstrike and set in the saloon for all the citizens of Goldstrike to see.

A barren sycamore was deemed an appropriate gallows and the end of Hunter's rope was thrown over a stout limb about twelve feet above the ground. The men were prepared to hoist him up but were stopped by Cage. "Not yet, men. We must give him time fer confession." Cage stepped up to him. He spoke softly. "I hear ya done well fer yerself here, Preacher. Shame ya can't take it with ya."

"You'll burn for eternity for killing Isabel."

"Bit late to be preachin'. Her sin be on your head, Preacher. Ya never should've involved her.

Now ya got a choice. We can hang ya real slow and gradual, or ya can confess to the murder and we'll just jerk ya up and be done with it."

Hunter clenched his jaw.

"You're a fool," Cage said. "Either way ya die."

Jak stepped forward and with a closed fist struck Hunter across the face, leaving a stream of blood trickling from his lip. "I'm told there's a commandment 'bout covetin' another man's wife, Preacher. I want ya ta rest easy knowin' I'll be takin' her back now."

Hunter spit out the blood that had pooled in his mouth. "You'll never find her."

"She just at th' boardin'house. Been there a week. I plan to collect her soon as we finish with ya." Jak smiled. "Woman knows where she stands round me. That's important. Ya should've learned that."

Jak's words sickened him. Why hadn't Quaye left? Hunter bowed his head and silently prayed, *God, if my years in your service have warranted anything, I beg you this one request. Take my life but keep her safe from him.* Even as he prayed, he recognized the futility of offering a life already lost to God.

Jak determined that Hunter was praying and, to Cage's displeasure, shouted, "I believe th' preacher here should give his own eulogy."

The mob roared in approval. Just then, a shotgun blast quieted the group. The men turned to see all eleven of the Chang family standing armed with axes, picks, four shotguns, and two of Hunter's rifles.

"Free Mister Bell," shouted Sonny. He leveled the rifle at Cage, who raised his hands and smiled flippantly as he stepped back. "Whoa, Johnny, we're just carryin' out the law. Ya don't want a be tanglin' with us." He glanced to the men and a few were already moving toward their guns. Hunter observed the action. There were too many men in the mob and the sentiment against the Chinese was too hot. If they somehow survived the encounter, the community of Bethel would run over them like a wave. They would all hang by nightfall.

Hunter shouted, "No, Sonny. You go back home. You take them away!"

Sonny looked at him quizzically and Hunter shouted to the vigilantes, "Let them be. They're just Chinamen."

The Chinese stood, not willing to desert their friend.

"I said go," Hunter shouted. "I killed the girl. I must hang for it. Go, now! *Dzou ba!* Go back to your home!"

Cage smiled. The Chinese had accomplished what he was unable to. Confused, all of the family but Sonny lowered their guns. Just then a shot rang out and Cage clutched his chest, dropped to his knees, and fell face forward into the snow near Hunter's feet. Jak ran to catch the end of the rope but a second shot clipped him in the chest and threw him backward.

"I'll kill the next man who goes for the rope." The heavily accented voice came from a one-armed man on horseback. He trotted slowly toward the group, his pistol held in his hand and the horse's reins clamped beneath the stub of the missing arm. Hunter recognized Isabel's father, Père Gayarre.

One of the Bethel vigilantes, unaware of the Cajun's prowess, drew on Gayarre, who mercifully shot the weapon out of his hands. Gayarre pointed his revolver at a man crouched over the dying Cage. "Cut loose the preacher."

The man quickly sliced the ropes that bound Hunter's hands with a buck knife. Hunter lifted the noose from around his neck.

"We would've let ya hang him," said one man.

Gayarre rode closer, his eyes blazing with vengeance. "Preacher didn't murder my daughter. Vigilantes did." He surveyed the group. "I should kill you all."

Still lying on his back, Jak shouted, "Ya cowards! There's only one a him and a hunderd of ya!"

Though Gayarre was outnumbered more than forty to one, such odds are of small comfort if you're the one to be killed. Gayarre was fast enough that he would undoubtedly take a handful of men with him. Not a man was willing to go for his gun.

The men from Bethel were the first to wander off. Several of them apologized to Hunter before they went. One of the Goldstrike vigilantes shouted, "It was Cage who done it. He got his." His confederates were quick to agree. They left Cage lying facedown in the trampled snow as they went back to their horses.

As the crowd dissipated, Hunter nodded to Gayarre, who only stared back with eyes dark with pain. Hunter meant nothing to him. Gayarre had come for Cage; his job was done.

Suddenly there was another shot. Hunter cried out then fell forward clutching his abdomen. On the ground behind him, Jak held a smoking pistol. The Cajun fired and Jak fell back, never to rise again.

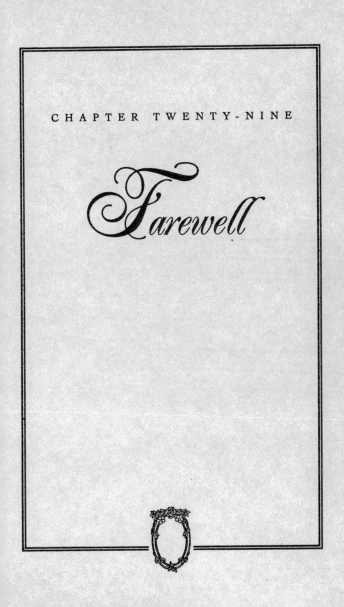

CHAPTER TWENTY-NINE

Farewell

$\mathcal{L}$ung Yan sat next to Hunter's bed with his head bowed. He was speaking softly in such melodic Mandarin as to resemble singing. The eldest of the Chang family, Lung Yan's eyebrows and hair were silver-gray. He wore a navy satin cap and a stiff, brocaded satin blouse. The room was dark and the glowing embers of the incense that surrounded the bed cast an eerie light on the healer's face.

Hunter's shirt had been stripped away. There was a poultice laid across his abdomen where the bullet had egressed, perforating the skin just below his rib. The ball had entered just below his kidney and had missed his vital organs, though it had caused internal bleeding and Hunter had passed out from the loss of blood and the exquisite pain. Hunter awoke to the pungent smell of lit incense. Lung Yan raised his head and spoke.

Sonny suddenly appeared next to the old man.

"Howdy, Mister Bell," he said.

"So I am not in the hereafter," he said sardonically.

Sonny did not understand.

"How am I?" Hunter asked.

"You stop bleeding."

Lung Yan lit a rice-paper tube resembling a thick cigar and he blew across it until the ash smoldered. He held the burning wick about an inch above Hunter's chest, rotating it slowly in his fingers.

"What is he doing?"

"To rid you of evil wind."

Hunter closed his eyes. Sonny asked abruptly, "You not kill the girl?"

"No."

"You tell lie to save us."

"Yes."

Sonny bowed to him. "You honorable man."

Hunter had no idea how long he had been lying there. He vaguely recalled the glow of the incense and the cold poultice laid on his skin, and remembered speaking with someone at length.

"How long have I been here?"

"Two days."

"Have I spoken?"

"You speak of Irishwoman," Sonny said.

"The Irishwoman."

"She come," Sonny said.

"Quaye?"

"She hold your hand this night."

"Where is she?"

"She outside. I get her for you?"

"Yes."

A few moments later Quaye knelt by the side of his bed, taking his hand in hers. Her eyes were red from crying.

"Why didn't you leave?" Hunter asked.

She wiped back a tear.

"Why, Quaye?"

Quaye sighed deeply. "You may have freed my soul, Hunter, but you have chained my heart."

Hunter squeezed her hand. "Finally, I did something right." He smiled, then suddenly grimaced with pain. "How long have you been with me?"

"As soon as I learned of your arrest. I was on my way to you when you were shot."

"Who shot me?"

"It was Jak." She added without emotion, "He's dead."

"How did Gayarre know?"

"Gayarre?"

"The Cajun. Isabel's father. How did he know I was innocent?"

"One of the vigilantes went to him."

"A vigilante with a conscience?"

"Cage had led the committee when they lynched his brother."

Hunter nodded with understanding. "Has a doctor seen me?"

"The doctor laid the bandage. He said the bullet passed right through you. There is nothing more to be done. Sonny brought Lung Yan."

They were silent for a moment and Quaye gently ran her fingers through his hair. "Just rest, my darling."

Sonny spoke softly to Lung Yan, who stood and took the glowing wormwood from Hunter's chest.

"We leave you, Mister Bell," Sonny said.

Hunter weakly lifted his hand and Sonny took it. "Thank you, Sonny. *Sye, sye.*"

"Hou hwei you chi," Sonny said without translating. The two left the room in silence. When they had departed Hunter asked, "Did I speak to you?"

Quaye nodded.

"Did I shame myself?"

She smiled and nodded again.

"At least you smile." He exhaled slowly. "It is strange. I do not know if I am going to live or die."

"You are going to live," Quaye said.

Hunter nodded. "I am thirsty."

"Then I will bring you water."

Quaye returned with a ladle full of cold water. She helped him raise his head and he drank, then laid his head back on the pillow. "What else can I do?"

"Talk to me. Help me forget the pain."

"Would you like me to read to you?"

"Yes. Read to me. Read to me from *our* book."

She walked to the shelf and retrieved his book of poems. She opened to the twentieth sonnet.

"Belovèd, my belovèd, when I think
That thou wast in the world a year ago,
What time I sate alone here in the snow
And saw no footprint, heard the silence sink
No moment at thy voice . . . but, link by link,
Went counting all my chains, as if that so
They never could fall off at any blow
Struck by thy possible hand . . . why, thus I drink
Of life's great cup of wonder! Wonderful, . . ."

She had not finished the book before Hunter fell asleep. She lifted the blanket up to his chest and leaned over and kissed his still lips.

The next day Hunter woke shortly before noon. Quaye had spent the night sleeping at his side in the rocking chair. She had woken before dawn and had watched him for more than an hour before she went to work straightening up the cabin and preparing coffee and food. When he woke she came to him. A shaft of sunlight shone through the bared window and as Quaye passed through it Hunter thought she looked like an angel. She sat down next to Hunter with a bowl of soup. He smiled when he saw her.

"Are you hungry?"

"Yes."

Quaye dipped the spoon into the bowl and held it to his lips. Hunter closed his mouth on the spoon, puckered, swallowed, then coughed. "What is that?"

Quaye smiled. "It is the soup Sonny brought."

"Whiskey is smoother."

"He assured me that it is good for you," Quaye said, again filling the spoon.

Hunter shook his head. "I prefer the bullet."

She smiled again. "I will get you some broth."

As she started to rise, Hunter took her hand. "Don't leave me."

She sat back down.

"If I am to live, there are matters to discuss."

"What matters, love?"

"Our future."

"Our future," she repeated. "How odd that it should sound so pleasant. I have never considered the future with any degree of desire."

"Then I will help you see it. I will help you dream." He took her hand. "We will sell our claim and when I am able we will take the first stage back to Pennsylvania. There is a place there that must be like Eden before the Fall, a small town in the Brandywine Valley along the banks of the Brandywine River called Chadds Ford. The hills are round and so lush that it almost hurts the eye. And there are great forests thick with black walnut and hickory and beech trees. There are apple and pear orchards that stretch as far as the eye can see. After the fall apple harvest the townspeople come together for a fair and dancing. We will buy the largest house in the county, a grand home with crystal chandeliers and tapestry floor carpets. And there will be a harp. Hannah will learn the harp. And she will have a large yard to run in and a walled garden to explore. She will have a pony and we will go on rides into the hills. You will have a coach and servants. I will give you everything you have ever been denied."

"Then I will have you?"

He suddenly turned serious. "If you will have me."

"You propose such to a widow of not a week?"

"I do."

"You are bold," she said lightly. "But I will have you."

"I am a bargain. You get not just me, but Hannah as well. You must have the both of us."

"Yes. And Hannah. We will be a family. I have wanted children, but I was unable to conceive with Jak. I thought it a blessing then, but now it is a curse." She looked sorrowful. "I want to bear your child, Hunter."

Hunter kissed her brow.

"We have Hannah," he said. "And we will fill her with enough love and dreams for a dozen children. What happiness we do not accomplish she will recompense with hers. And when we are gray and old, Hannah will play her harp for us while our grandchildren crawl at our feet."

Quaye sighed. "You are a splendid escort of dreams." Hunter tried to pull her closer but it hurt him too much. Quaye climbed into the bed next to him. Their mouths met and Quaye thought she wanted nothing more than this man. When they parted, she again sighed as she nestled her face next to his. "I surrender my heart to you, my love. I will follow you wherever you go. To whatever dream you sail."

Hunter smiled and their noses touched. "You are my vessel to reach such lofty dreams. Such beauty shines in sable skies as a star one might sail a ship by. Or to not sail at all, but drift without harbor in tranquil swells of utter contentment."

"And what book is that from?"

Hunter smiled and kissed her face. "Just my heart." Then he leaned back and groaned softly.

"You must rest. Rest, my love. I will be your warmth."

He pulled her head into his chest as he lay back into the pillow and Quaye listened to his pounding heart slow as he drifted back to sleep. While he slept she envisioned the rolling hills of the Brandywine Valley, the winding river with pastel meadow flowers bent over its banks, gazing at their own reflection as Narcissus's children. She pictured Hannah, the Hannah of the photograph, and saw her come to life, her chestnut curls bouncing as she played, squealing with childhood joy. She closed her eyes and, in his warmth, let the music of the dream serenade her to sleep.

It was late that afternoon that Hunter moaned

loudly, waking them both from sleep. His forehead was beaded with perspiration.

"What is the matter, darling?" she asked, taking his hand.

He raised her hand to his cheek. It burned with fever. She climbed out of the bed and dipped a rag into the water bucket at his side and gently patted his forehead. He opened his eyes and gazed at her. In his eyes she saw something unspeakable. Hunter whispered, "Quaye."

"Yes, darling?"

"I know now."

"You know what, darling?"

"If I am to live or die."

His hand went to his stomach, gently rested on the hot flesh. The area around his wound was inflamed and bright, and red streaks climbed upward toward his chest. Quaye looked into his fever-dimmed eyes and understood his meaning. She lifted her hand to her mouth.

"I am sorry."

Quaye clasped her hands together around his. "No, Hunter. Please don't leave me."

"It is God's will."

"Then I will pray to Him." She fell to her knees at the side of the bed and bowed her head. "Please don't take him. I will give you anything. Anything but him."

Hunter squeezed her hand. "Quaye," he said lovingly. "Learn from me. Pray His will be done, not ours."

Her hand trembled and her eyes were wide and wet. "I fear His will."

"It is not to be feared." He moved his tongue over his parched lips. "My love, bring me the purse on the shelf. It is near my diary. Bring it to me."

She went to the shelf and found the brown leather purse closed with a drawstring and brought it back, not understanding why he needed it. Inside was a pen and two pieces of paper folded into squares; one was inscribed, the other blank. He scrawled something on the written page then handed both papers to Quaye.

"The claim is now in your name. Record what I say."

"Hunter, not now. . . ."

"You must go to Mr. Wharton at the boarding-house. Tell him that you have the claim. . . ."

Quaye's face hardened. "No. Do not speak such. You will do so when you are well."

"Quaye, I must speak now, love. There is not much time."

His words pierced her as sharply as daggers, but as she gazed into his eyes she knew that she must obey. He lifted his hand and caressed her cheek. "You must live our dream, Quaye."

She bit back her tears. "Hunter . . ."

"Tell Wharton that you will accept his offer. Tell him there are conditions. He must protect the Changs' claim. He must put it in writing."

Quaye scrawled the words.

"Tell him that your money is to be sent to the Chester County Bank. I have a friend there. Parley Smythe. You may trust him."

As Quaye wrote, her tears fell on the page, blurring the words. She stopped and began to sob and he reached for her.

"You saved me, why can't I save you?"

His love for her shone through his pained eyes. "But you did, my love." He took a labored breath. "I am at peace with my God." He wiped away Quaye's tears. "Do not weep for me. I am a blessed man. I have felt true love twice in my life. It is more than any man should hope for."

Quaye held his hand to her cheek.

"Will you take Hannah, Quaye? Will you finish what I failed to do?"

She nodded. "Yes."

"When she is old enough to understand, would you tell her that her father loved her. There is a sealed letter in the book of sonnets. Have you seen it?"

Quaye lay her head against his chest. "Yes. It will be done, my love."

"I so wish to give you my name. I would have us marry. Does it seem foolish to you?"

She could not speak but shook her head.

"Could you take my name, just to lose me?"

Quaye squeezed his hand tightly. "To lose you a thousand times over."

Hunter stroked her cheek. "Yes, you are brave."

Quaye removed her Claddaugh ring and placed it in Hunter's hand. "Marry us. God will honor your words."

He closed his hand around hers and closed his eyes, then opened them and looked on her longingly. "My sweet Quaye." He swallowed. "I take you as wedded wife and pledge my troth, to cherish you according to the ordinance of God in the holy bond of marriage.

"Do you take me to be your wedded husband, and pledge your troth, to cherish me according to the ordinance of God?"

"I do."

"I promise before God to be your loving and faithful husband, in joy and in sorrow, in sickness and in health, till death . . ." He stopped at the word and again closed his eyes. ". . . For as long as a merciful God may grant us in the eternities."

He held the ring to his view, then he turned it inward.

"It is as my mother said," Quaye said. "We have fulfilled her wish."

Richard Paul Evans

Hunter squeezed her hand. "With this ring, in token of our abiding love, I thee wed; in the name of the Father; and of the Son; and of the Holy Spirit." He placed the ring on her finger. "By the authority committed unto me as a minister of the church of Jesus Christ I declare us married. What God hath joined together, let no man put asunder."

"My husband," Quaye said. She buried her head in Hunter's shoulder and he held her as she wept. Then Hunter lay his hand on Quaye's head, crushing and twining her auburn hair between his fingers. His voice quivered as he began to speak. "I love thee with a love I seemed to lose/With my lost saints,—I love thee with the breath,/Smiles, tears, of all my life!—and . . ." He struggled for breath. Quaye lifted her head and looked at him fearfully. It was several minutes before his breathing calmed and he was again quiet. She pressed her cheek against his, her mouth to his ear, and, in a whisper, finished his verse, ". . . if God so choose,/I shall but love thee better after death."

There was no more sound but his ragged breathing and the fire's crackling. Quaye pressed her body into his, holding on to him as tightly as if she could stop his soul's flight.

It was hours later, somewhere in the unkept minutes of the night, that Hunter's chest rose, as if drawn forth by some spectral power, then fell back and he breathed no more. All alone, Quaye called out his name. Then she fell onto him and sobbed as if her heart would break.

CHAPTER THIRTY

The
Redemption

$\mathcal{T}$he elegant, slipper-shaped phaeton stopped in front of a redbrick mansion on the end of a red cobbled West Chester road. The top-hatted black coachman shouted to the horses then pulled the brake and climbed down from the box. He propped a step beneath the carriage door, opened the door, took Quaye's hand, and helped her out. She was dressed as fine as any of the society ladies of Philadelphia, wearing a black satin cape lined with apricot-colored satin and trimmed with black lace against the chill of early spring.

"This be the house, ma'am," the driver said.

"Thank you, Morris," Quaye said as she stepped out of the carriage. It was a large home, immaculately landscaped, with a bright flower garden of elecampane, gilly, star-shaped borage, and silver-stemmed, yellow-budded rue. Twenty yards north of the house was a small, fenced cemetery. Two bronze cupid sentries guarded the stone step entryway that led to the home's tiled porch.

Quaye felt as if she stood before a shrine. This had been Hunter's home. The house had been willed to the church two years before Hunter began his ministry by a wealthy widow. The top floor was used as the minister's lodging, while the rest of the house was used for Christian service: as a home for foster children and those in need.

A portly gray-haired woman in an apron peered out the door. Then she opened it all the way and hurriedly waddled down the porch to greet her visitor. A broad smile blanketed her wide, red-cheeked face as she extended her arms to Quaye.

"Sister Bell," she exclaimed. "I am Sister Folland." She embraced Quaye. "How was your journey?" She frowned. "Oh, how foolish of me to ask of such an arduous journey. You must be exhausted."

"It was quite tolerable," Quaye said. "Thank you for asking. Traveling east is much less strenuous than traveling west."

The woman raised her eyebrows. "How so?"

"Each stop has more conveniences than the previous, so one is constantly feeling blessed."

"How right you are, dear." The woman smiled then placed her hand on Quaye's back. "We have so looked forward to your arrival and making your acquaintance."

"As I have looked forward to making yours. I trust that the legal work is complete."

"Yes, Sister. There were a few minor technicalities, but Mr. Smythe at the bank was of great assistance. He always was such a dear and loyal friend to Minister Bell."

"He has been very helpful."

"Your generosity to the church held great sway with the church officers."

Quaye lowered her voice. "Does she know of my coming?"

"We have not spoken with her. We thought it best for the child that you meet her first. Just in case there had been a change of . . ." she chose the word carefully, "circumstance."

"There has been no change."

The woman smiled again. "Praise be to God," she said, raising her hands. "Please follow me, Sister Bell." The women went inside the mansion and Quaye was led down a long hallway into a parlor where a small girl sat alone on the floor playing with a cloth doll. She looked up at Quaye's entrance. When Quaye saw her it brought a powerful wave of emotion. She was Hunter's child, evident in all her features. But most true to her father were her eyes. They were as deep and piercing as Hunter's and when Quaye looked into them it made her heart swell with love.

"I would like to visit with Hannah," Quaye said.

"Of course, Sister Bell. I will be in the kitchen. May I bring you some tea?"

"No, thank you."

When the woman left the room, Quaye crouched down next to the little girl. "Hello, Hannah."

The girl timidly looked up. "Hello."

"Does your doll have a name?"

"Her name is Rachel." Hannah struggled with buttoning the doll's dress.

"May I play with you?"

The girl nodded.

Quaye sat and arranged her skirts around her. "Maybe I can help you with that dress." Hannah offered her the doll and Quaye finished buttoning its dress then handed it back to Hannah. "Rachel is very pretty."

"What is your name?" she asked.

"My name is Quaye."

"I have never heard that name."

"My name comes from a place far away. Across the sea."

"I am not allowed near the water," Hannah said thoughtfully.

Quaye smiled. "Perhaps when you are bigger."

"Is your home across the sea?"

"My home is in the next township."

Hannah changed her mind about the dress and

began to unbutton it. "What is your home like?"

"It is lovely. It has tall white posts and a fountain. There is a guest cottage and stables. And there is a beautiful garden with many flowers. And fields with wildflowers."

"I like flowers," Hannah said. "Miss Folland spanked me because I picked the flowers in the bed."

"There are many meadow flowers for you to pick at my house." She gently touched the girl's arm. "Hannah, would you like to come see my house?"

The girl did not look up, but nodded. "Can Rachel and Samantha come?"

"Yes. Is Samantha also a doll?"

She shook her head. "Samantha is a tree."

Quaye smiled again. "I will have to see how tall Samantha is. There are many trees at my house."

"We are having dumplings for dinner at my house," Hannah said.

"Do you like dumplings?"

The girl nodded. "Can you stay for dinner?"

"I must go back to my home tonight. Would it be all right if I come back tomorrow?"

Hannah nodded.

"Then I will see you tomorrow. Good-bye, Hannah."

"Good-bye, Miss Quaye."

Quaye looked into the little girl's eyes. "May I hold you?"

Hannah nodded coyly. Quaye took the little girl in her arms and held her tightly, tears streaked down her cheeks.

When they parted Hannah asked, "Why are you crying?"

"I am just very happy to see you."

Quaye kissed her, then rose and walked out of the room. Sister Folland met her in the hallway.

"Your visit went well?"

"Yes. It went well," Quaye said. "It is enough for today. I will be back tomorrow."

"I think you are wise in taking your time."

"I know what it is like to be taken from one's home," Quaye said.

Sister Folland escorted Quaye outside. On the walk to the carriage Quaye noticed the small cemetery obscured by the building's shadow. "Sister Folland, is that where Rachel is buried?"

"Yes, my dear."

"Do you mind if I visit her grave?"

"Not at all."

Quaye walked toward the tiny fenced cemetery. In the east corner was a slim, soapstone headstone. It was a humble marker, rounded at the top, with a cross chiseled above the name.

RACHEL BELL
April 16, 1832–August 1, 1853

Quaye removed her bonnet and the spring wind pulled tendrils from her carefully arranged hair. She pulled several strands back from her face then crossed herself and knelt before the stone, her head slightly bowed in prayer. Then she raised her eyes and touched the stone's cold face, slowly running her fingers across the engraved words.

"I feel that you are my sister, Rachel. For only you and I know what it is to be loved by him. And to love him. I will do my best to raise Hannah as you would have. I will not let her forget you or him. I promise you."

Quaye rose and walked back to the carriage. She said to Sister Folland, "I will never adequately be able to thank you for all that you have done. Hunter spoke so fondly of you."

At the mention of the minister's name the woman's brow furrowed. "Sister Bell, forgive me, but if I might ask . . ." Her eyes showed her reticence but Quaye smiled reassuringly, coaxing the words from her. "Before he went, did Pastor Bell come again to God?"

Quaye touched her arm and smiled. "I don't think he ever left."

The woman smiled. "Praise the Lord God Almighty." She embraced Quaye.

"I will see you tomorrow noon," Quaye said.

Sister Folland took her hand. "God's speed, Sister Bell."

The coachman opened Quaye's door and helped her in. He then climbed atop the buckboard and shouted to the horses. Sister Folland watched the carriage grow small in the distance then went back inside to tend to her chores.

❉

Quaye made the drive from Chadds Ford every day to visit Hannah. Each day, Quaye extended the length of her stay, until, after the second week, the two spent nearly the whole of every day together. As Quaye fell in love with the girl, Hannah fell in love with her. The child instinctively sensed that there was something different about this new visitor than the other women who had come in and out of her short life; that somehow Quaye was more to her than Sister Folland and the other church women.

Quaye did not know when she would take the child back to her home in Chadds Ford. She was in no hurry. As she had told Sister Folland, she had known what it was like to be torn from a home. She also believed that she would know when it was the right time, for she felt that there was divinity in her mission. She did not seek to rush the divine.

On a cool June morning, six and a half weeks since her first visit, Quaye was kneeling in the church garden planting zinnias with Hannah crouched by her side. As Quaye plied the black earth between her fingers, laying the seeds and patting the soil back with her hand, Hannah was unusually quiet; as thoughtful as a four-year-old child sometimes is. Suddenly she felt Hannah's troubled gaze upon her. Quaye smiled up at her.

"What is it, sweetheart?" The child looked at her nervously. Quaye set aside a small trowel, brushed the dirt off her hands, and pulled Hannah close. "What is wrong?"

Hannah looked earnestly into Quaye's face. "Will you be my mother?"

A broad smile crossed Quaye's face as she held the child and wept. That same day Hannah's bags were packed into the phaeton and she drove off with Quaye. The little girl stared out the carriage window as they rode on crooked country roads past thickly wooded forests and large farms and well-kept fields with trellises of grapes set by boxwood hedges. They passed orchards of pears, and apples of all varieties: Jonathan, McIntosh, Lodi, Empire, Rome, Nittany, and York Imperial.

After about an hour, the carriage approached a magnificent home on a lush knoll rising above a fifty-acre orchard. The home was pale yellow with white-framed windows and tall black shutters. It had a steep hipped roof of black shingles, with four tall brick chimneys, one located at each corner of the house. A portico above the front door was supported by two Corinthian columns, with a decorative parapet with intricate gold-leaf fretwork panels. Parallel to the roadway stretched a tall white fence leading to a broad center gateway adorned with brick posts with finials carved of rose granite.

Hannah peered out the carriage window as they entered through the front gate and circled a fountained roundabout.

"This is our home," Quaye said.

When the carriage had stopped and Quaye had helped her out, Hannah ran to the front door. The interior of the house was still more impressive than its exterior. The ceilings were tall, slightly above ten feet high, and the foyer rose two stories above the marble floor entryway. A chandelier of brass and Strauss crystal hung in the center of the foyer over an elliptical staircase. Visible from the foyer was a large, crimson-walled sitting room with an elaborate tapestry carpet and a gold-leaf harp next to a mahogany fall-front desk. On the wall behind the desk was an unfinished portrait of a young man. Hannah stared at the painting.

"It is your father," Quaye said.

Hannah gazed at it for a moment, then Quaye

took her hand and they climbed the stairway. The first door on the second floor was a small boudoir with a marble-front fireplace with brass andirons shaped like greyhounds. In the center of the room was a child-size canopied bed with ivory lace drapes and mahogany bedposts. A porcelain doll lay in the center of the bed on its peach quilt.

"This is your bedroom," Quaye said. Hannah looked around in wonder. On a small chest of drawers was a miniature carousel with intricately painted pastel and gilt menagerie animals with a small flag atop its canopy. Just a few feet from it was a small fruitwood bookshelf filled to capacity with picture books. A wooden chest lay on the floor next to it, its top lifted to reveal a collection of richly dressed dolls. She walked over and picked up a bisque-faced baby doll, clutching it to her chest.

In the corner of the room was an oblong floor mirror set on an ornately carved and gilded wood frame. Carrying her doll, Hannah walked to it and stared at her reflection, watched the image mimic her own movement. After a moment she looked up at Quaye. "That is me," she said softly.

Quaye gently put her arms around Hannah and stared with her at the reflection, then pulled her close. "Welcome home, my dear sweet girl."

And perhaps she spoke as much to herself as she did to the child.

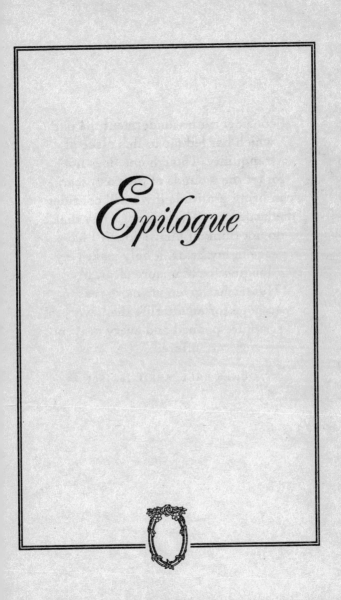

Epilogue

"I consider with wonderment the path which has led me to this place of tranquility. Though one does not forget the wounds of the past, scars can bring gratitude if we will consider the healer. . . . There is not a day that I do not think of him. Though I have peace in my heart, it only makes my longing for him more clear. My Hunter has given me more reason to hope for an afterlife than every scripture penned and every prayer offered."

❋ QUAYE BELL, APRIL 16, 1901 ❋

*W*hen Hannah was old enough to concern herself with such things, she questioned her mother as to why she never remarried, as there were always men who wished to court her. Quaye smiled sadly and replied she had been married twice and it was enough for one lifetime. In her heart she thought a more truthful answer would have been that she had been married only once, and it was enough for all time.

Quaye believed that there would be a sign for the right moment to tell Hannah about her father. When Hannah was sixteen she discovered the shattered silver looking glass with its few remaining shards of glass, a necklace of jade beads, and the book of poetry. She asked her mother about them. Quaye led her to the parlor where they sat beneath Hunter's portrait while Quaye told her about her father and mother, and about an obscure western gold camp called Bethel. Then Quaye gave her the letter that Hunter had written. Hannah broke its seal and read it silently. Quaye held her as she wept.

As Hunter had once dreamed, Hannah learned to play the harp. Quaye would often sit in the parlor as the sun fell and listen to her daughter play, losing herself in the instrument's seraphic melodies. Sometimes mother and daughter would walk hand in hand through their property and talk of days past. On serene winter nights, Hannah would lay her head in her mother's lap as Quaye would read passages from Hunter's diary. These were the times that they felt Hunter most near.

The summer of Hannah's twenty-first year, Hannah, like her mothers, married a minister. The morning of the wedding ceremony Quaye took from her hand the Claddaugh ring and bequeathed it to her daughter as her mother once had for her.

Hannah and her husband moved to a new home and congregation in eastern Massachusetts where she bore and raised three children in sight of Duxbury bay—two boys and a rust-haired girl. The older boy they named Hunter, the younger Connall, and the girl they named Faith.

Only after Hannah was gone did Quaye return to Ireland and again walk Cobh harbor and the marsh banks of the River Lee. The memories of her girlhood came back as strong and resonant as the chime from the bells of Shandon. The town and its people were different. They had healed, but the land had not. For the land does not forget. As Quaye walked the paths of her youth she felt the presence of spirits rising from the silent bogs and heard their cry in every breeze that swept through the midnight forests and misted glens.

She visited the old clachan with its remnant stone walls and reclaimed homes and fields and found them occupied by a new generation of Irish, worked by hands younger than hers, by Irish who had only heard of the land's betrayal.

She found the hovel where she had been born. She stood in the very place she had the night that Jak came for her. And she learned for fact that what Hunter had supposed of her father—what she had followed in faith—indeed had been the truth all along. Her brother had died the very week of her departure. Her parents had lived only one month more. Alone, beneath the gray canopy of the Irish sky, she knelt and kissed their graves and thanked them for her life.

Quaye returned to Chadds Ford. She lived long enough to see her posterity grow and hold not just Hannah's children, but Hannah's grandchildren. Though Hannah never ceased to implore her to come to Massachusetts and reside with her beneath the same roof, Quaye remained until the end of her life at the banks of the Brandywine, content to walk alone in its lush valley and remember the desert where she had found love.

Bethel died. By the turn of the century the gold was gone and the people left with it, leaving behind the wooden skeletons of a once flourishing township and the memory of what had transpired there.

And perhaps the name given Bethel in irony was appropriate after all. For what was true for Hunter and Quaye is true for all: that the salvation of man is only in and through love. And where there is love, there God resides.

Quaye died in her home in 1915. Upon her death, her estate was willed to the church and was used to shelter women in need. She had asked little for herself in this life and on her death she had but two requests. That she be buried next to her husband in the deserted, weed-filled cemetery in Bethel. And in her hands was to be placed the sterling silver looking glass.

A
gift for my readers

Over the years, I have received many requests for
a compilation of material from my works—
quotations, diary entries, and thoughts from the
characters who populate my novels.

I am pleased to now make available

THE QUOTABLE EVANS
*Diary Entries, Letters, and Lessons from the novels
of Richard Paul Evans*

To order a free copy, please email me at:

www.richardpaulevans.com

or send your name and mailing address to:

Richard Paul Evans
P.O. Box 1416
Salt Lake City, UT 84110

Copies will be available as long as supplies last.
There is no charge for the booklet or the shipping
and handling.

Thank you for your continued interest and support.

Other timeless classics
from *New York Times*
bestselling author

Richard Paul Evans

— ⊱❈⊰ —

The Christmas Box Collection

— ⊱❈⊰ —

The Locket

— ⊱❈⊰ —

Timepiece

Visit
❖ Pocket Books ❖
online at

....

www.SimonSays.com

....

Keep up on the latest new
releases from your favorite
authors, as well as author
appearances, news, chats,
special offers and more.

SIMON & SCHUSTER
A VIACOM COMPANY
www.SimonSays.com

Pocket
Books

2381-01